Sabin loathes the desert, which makes living in Hell the opposite of fun. Luckily for him, he can avoid the sand and the heat as long as he stays in the palace, and with as much work as he does for Berith, he doesn't plan to leave anytime soon.

Until Berith orders him to.

Zeno is a loner, and for good reason. He's known as The Mercenary, and he's Hell's bogeyman. People are afraid of him, and he's fine with that because it means they leave him alone.

But when Zeno stumbles onto a convoy attacked by a group of demons, he stupidly decides to step in. He ends up saddled with a pretty palace boy, Sabin, and agrees to take him back to the palace—for a price, of course.

Neither of them expects to fall for the other, but they soon realize it's not impossible. What is impossible is for them to find a way to make things work between them. Sabin belongs in the palace, while Zeno belongs to the desert.

How can they be together?

A Demon's Opportunity
Copyright © 2022 Catherine Lievens
ISBN: 978-1-4874-3634-6
Cover art by Angela Waters

Published by eXtasy Books Inc

Look for us online at:
www.eXtasybooks.com

A Demon's Opportunity
Demons Destinies 3

By

Catherine Lievens

CHAPTER ONE

Sabin was doing his best to ignore the scene in front of him, but it wasn't easy when Berith and Mel were all over each other. They weren't doing anything inappropriate, but Sabin couldn't avoid listening to them. Mel was in Berith's lap, and they were cuddling, for fuck's sake. Why were they cuddling in Sabin's office?

Mel sighed heavily. "I should go. Class will start soon."

"I don't think the kids will care if you're a little late," Berith said.

"They won't, but I will."

Sabin heard them shuffling around, and he risked looking up. He was relieved to see Mel had gotten up and was straightening his clothes. He caught Sabin's gaze and smiled, and Sabin couldn't help smiling back.

He may never fully understand why Berith had fallen for the human, but Mel was a good person, much better than Sabin had expected. He deserved to be happy, and apparently, Berith made him happy.

"Sorry about that," Mel said. His cheeks were flushed, which was kind of endearing.

"Not a problem. It wasn't your fault, anyway." When Mel had come in to tell Berith he was going to work, Berith had pulled him into his lap. Mel had tried to protest, no doubt on Sabin's behalf, but when Berith wanted something, he got it. It was one of the perks of being a prince of Hell, Sabin supposed.

"How am I supposed to resist this man?" Berith asked as

he caught Mel's hand and kissed its palm.

Mel flushed deeper. "You're a smooth talker, but I really need to go. Besides, you have work to do."

"I'll see you for lunch?"

"Of course."

Mel leaned closer, and Sabin looked away as he and Berith kissed. It was odd to see Berith act like this with anyone, let alone a human. Berith wasn't the worst prince of Hell, not even close, but he'd never been this soft. He was behaving this way only because Sabin and Mel were the only people around, but still. Sabin had never seen this side of his friend and boss until the human had appeared, and while he was glad Berith was happy, he still didn't know what to think of all of this.

The sound of his office door opening and closing made him look up. Mel was gone, and only Berith was left in his chair on the other side of Sabin's desk. He'd linked his fingers together on his stomach, and he was staring at Sabin.

Sabin schooled his expression. "Are you done cuddling Mel?"

"Unfortunately. What were you thinking just now?"

"That you're annoying."

"Is that right? You do know that most princes of Hell would have your head for saying something like that, right?"

"And I should care why? You're not most princes of Hell. You won't stick me in the dungeon just because of what I said."

Berith laughed. "You're lucky I love you."

Sabin was, although he'd die rather than acknowledge that right now. Besides, Berith knew he was aware of it. "Are you finally ready to go to work?"

Berith waved at Sabin to start talking. "I'm listening."

Sabin went over the latest numbers on how much the palace spent every day and how much it earned. He had detailed charts, but Berith never wanted to see them. He trusted his

2

accountants, and they'd never betray him. They were very much aware of what would happen to them if they did.

Berith might be one of the nicest princes of Hell, but it didn't mean he wasn't a demon. Besides, Sabin kept an eye on them. He wasn't nearly as trusting as Berith.

"All of this is boring," Berith lamented. "Can I go now?"

"Depends. What are you planning on doing? Work, or spying on Mel while he's working?"

Berith's expression told Sabin he'd nailed it. He *had* been planning to spy on Mel.

Sabin shook his head. Sometimes he didn't recognize his friend. It wasn't a bad thing, because Berith was happy, more so than Sabin had ever seen him, but it could become a problem if other princes of Hell and demons realized what was happening. They might not attack Berith head-on, but they wouldn't hesitate to try to take out Mel. Mel was human, and he wouldn't be able to defend himself.

Although he'd had to defend himself the last time a demon attacked him. He'd used a vase, and while it wouldn't have been enough to kill the demon, it had bought Mel enough time for people to notice what was happening and run to protect him.

"What will you do once you're on the road and you can't spy on him all the time?" Sabin asked as he stacked his files together.

"What are you talking about?"

Sabin stared. "You can't tell me you don't remember. We've been talking about it for weeks."

"Tell me again, then."

"You have to get on the road soon to visit your vassals."

It was an unfortunate but necessary job. Every few years, Berith visited the people who lived in his territories. He listened to what they had to say, made lists of things they needed, and ensured they got those things. It kept people happy, and it made sure they didn't betray Berith or move on to another prince. The princes of Hell were some of the most powerful demons in Hell, and they were always trying to kill each other. Berith mostly managed to stay out of the way, but sometimes even he was targeted. Keeping his people happy meant he didn't have to worry about them betraying him.

Berith groaned. "It's that time already?"

"It is, and you'd know it if you listened to me when I talk."

"I can't leave the palace."

"Well, too bad, because you're going to have to. You know this is necessary."

"But I can't leave Mel and my family on their own. It's too dangerous, and it's just as dangerous for them to come with me. No, I can't leave."

"You're going to have to."

"We'll find a way around this."

"Will we? Well, I'm listening. What solution do you think you can find?"

Berith scowled. The problem with that was that Sabin wasn't afraid of him, and he scowled right back. They stared at each other until Berith sighed and his expression smoothed out.

"I know it's necessary, but I don't think I can do it this year. It's way too soon to leave Mel on his own."

"He wouldn't be on his own. Cyarea and Aloise aren't going anywhere, and there are plenty of guards at the palace."

Unfortunately, Sabin would have to travel with Berith. He hated the desert, the dust, and the temperature, but just like Berith didn't have a way out of this, he didn't, either.

He wasn't the only one. Lon would be traveling with them, too, to make sure Berith was protected. It meant fewer guards would be at the palace, but they'd still be leaving a good number of them behind. Enough guards would be present for Berith not to have to worry, although Sabin understood why he did. Lately, too many demons had managed to sneak into the palace up to the private wing and attack either him or Mel.

Lon had been working overtime to find out how they got in, but apart from one servant who let one of the demons in, they hadn't found anything. There had to be more people behind it, working with Berith's enemies, and maybe it would be a good thing for Berith to be away from the palace for a bit.

Or maybe it wouldn't be.

There was no way to know what the demons trying to kill Berith would do. Would they come after him and try to kill him on the road, or would they target the people he left behind? Sabin didn't have to ask to know this was what Berith was worried about. There was no way out of going, though. Berith had to get on the road and visit the people in his territory, and he had to do it soon.

Berith shook his head. "I don't care how many guards are at the palace. I'm not leaving my family."

Sabin could tell it would be useless to insist that he had to. Berith was stubborn on the best of days, and when his family was concerned, even more so. Sabin would just have to continue organizing the trip, and by the time he was done and ready to leave, Berith would be, too.

Or at least, Sabin hoped so. He wasn't in the mood to deal with a princely tantrum, and he doubted he would be when the time came for them to leave.

Zeno kept an eye on the group of demons walking ahead of him. He didn't think they'd realized they were being followed, which was how he liked things. He had a reputation to maintain, after all.

There were still too many people around for him to do what he needed to do. He'd been hired to get back something the demons had stolen, but he couldn't take it from them while they were still in town. No, it was better for him to wait until they walked out into the desert, which they were about to do. The four demons were headed toward one of the doors

5

in the walls surrounding the town that were closed during the night, and they stepped through without hesitating.

They should know better. They didn't know they were being followed, but still. Everyone was safer when they stayed in town.

But this played to Zeno's advantage.

He followed the demons in the desert. He didn't step through the door like they had because he needed to be discrete and make sure no one noticed him. Following people in towns or in the desert was something he'd trained to do, but it still wasn't easy. There were no places to hide out here, which meant one of the demons might see him. Luckily, they were too busy talking, pushing each other, and laughing. They were thieves, riding the high of another successful job.

Zeno didn't care what they did for a living. They lived in Hell, and they did what they had to in order to survive. But he'd been hired to get back one of the things they'd stolen, and he suspected they wouldn't give it to him just because he asked.

He continued following them until they were far enough from the town that no one would come running if they heard a fight. Then he made sure his hood concealed him, and cleared his throat.

One of the demons jumped, twirled around, and unsheathed a knife from his waist. He held it out, ready to kill anyone who he thought might be attacking him. Zeno stood a bit away, having suspected something like that would happen.

"Who the fuck are you?" the demon asked with a growl.

"I was hired to get back one of the things you stole. Give it to me, and I'll let you go without hurting you."

One of the other demons burst out laughing. "Are you serious? We're four against one. We're going to kick your ass, and that's the only thing you'll get."

Zeno had expected that, too, although he'd hoped it

wouldn't happen. But most demons were idiots. These weren't any different, especially considering who they'd robbed. Nybbas worked for Lucifer himself.

Zeno sighed as the mouthy demon threw himself at him. He stepped aside, grabbed the demon's neck, and pulled him back. The demon made a strangled sound, but Zeno wasn't done. He used his hold on the demon's neck to pull him closer, grabbed his head with both hands, and twisted.

The demon's body fell to the ground. A cloud of black dust rose around it, but Zeno was already focused on the others. They were staring at him with wide eyes, and he hoped that seeing their friend die would push them into doing the right thing.

He should have known he wouldn't be so lucky.

The demon who'd taken out his knife screamed and threw himself at Zeno. The knife slashed Zeno's forearm, but Zeno barely reacted beyond a hiss of pain. He grabbed the demon's wrist, twisted the demon's arm, and stabbed him with his own knife that he was still holding. Zeno knew precisely where to hit so that the wound would be deadly, so he wasn't surprised when the demon fell to his knees, then face-first in the dust. He left the knife where it was, since he didn't need it, and turned toward the last two demons.

They were staring at him with wide eyes and gaping mouths. He waited, knowing it wasn't over. Sure enough, one of the demons ran toward him. This one had a sword, which made Zeno snort. Did the demon think it would be easier to kill him with a sword? The sword was heavy, and if anything, it was harder for the demon to wield it.

Zeno effortlessly danced out of the way of the blade. He got behind the demon before the demon could realize what was happening, grabbed his head with both hands, and twisted.

The demon fell to the ground.

That left only one of them, and Zeno turned to face him. He

snorted when he saw that the demon had started running away as if he thought it would save him. He should have known better. Zeno took out one of his knives, took aim, and threw it at the demon's back. It sank between the demon's shoulders, and the demon went down like a stone.

Zeno sighed. He'd only wanted the thing he'd been paid to get back, dammit. He could have done without killing the demons if only they'd been smart enough to give him back what he wanted.

But they hadn't, and now he needed to search their bodies. He crouched next to the closest one and went through the demon's pockets. He found gold and a few knickknacks he suspected the demon had stolen in town. He left all of it there. He didn't need it, and he wasn't a thief. Once he was done with the first demon, he moved on to the one who'd attacked him with a knife. There was nothing of importance in his pockets or the pockets of the first demon he'd killed.

Zeno got to his feet, looked at the demon who'd run, and sighed. He disliked the desert, dammit, and he could have done without traipsing around it to get what he needed.

But Zeno needed to get to him, since the last demon had the thing Zeno was looking for, as well as Zeno's knife embedded in his back.

His footsteps raised small clouds of black dust that would have made him cough if his face hadn't been protected. When he reached the demon, he crouched next to him, took his knife out of the demon's back, and cleaned it on the demon's shirt. The demon groaned, a sure sign he wasn't dead, but Zeno didn't stop to ask him how he was. He rolled the demon onto his back and searched his pockets until he found what he was looking for.

He raised it and took a good look at it. He had no idea what was in the delicately carved wooden box and hadn't asked. It wasn't his job to know what he was taking back, just to take it back. It was one of the reasons people hired him, and he'd made a point of being discreet.

He got to his feet, pocketed both the knife and the box, and stepped away. A hand wrapped around his ankle, stopping him. He looked down at the demon, wondering what he wanted now. There was blood dripping from the demon's lips, and his eyes were wide and already clouding over.

"Save me," the demon croaked. "Take me back to town."

Zeno shook off the demon's hand. It would be too late for him even if Zeno managed to get him to town. It was too late for him now. He was dying, and nothing anyone could do would help him.

Zeno walked away. He left the demons there for whatever found them and wanted to eat them. It was the circle of life, or something like that. He was just doing his job, and he was damn good at it. If the demons had just listened and given him what he wanted, they wouldn't be bleeding out in the sand.

Zeno looked up at the sun. He still had enough time today to go back to the small town, find Nybbas, and get his money. He'd use it to buy more food so he'd have plenty when he headed out to go back home. Maybe he'd get a room in a tavern somewhere, rest a day or two.

He shook his head. No, he'd be better off once he was on the road headed home. He never did well around people.

"I already told you I'm not going," Berith said.

Sabin stared at him. "I heard you. You have to see it's not possible. You're the prince of this territory. People want to see you, talk to you, and complain to you. It's tradition, and you can't just decide not to go."

Berith waved Sabin's words away. "Who cares about tradition?"

"I realize you don't, but most of the people in your territory do. They've been expecting you and have been prepping for your presence. They've been waiting to tell you all their problems and beg you to solve them. Do you really want them to go to one of the other princes? Because you know what will happen if they do." It would be a sign that Berith was weak and couldn't take care of his people, which would be a sign that one of the other princes of Hell could attack and try to take Berith's territory.

That wasn't something any of them wanted.

Berith crossed his arms over his chest. There was a stubborn tilt to his jaw, and Sabin knew he wouldn't be able to convince him. He understood where Berith was coming from, but everyone had to do things they didn't want to do, including him. Berith had to know that pouting and deciding to stay back wouldn't help anyone, right? It certainly wouldn't help Mel, because if Berith was seen as weak, the palace would be attacked, and that was where Mel lived.

"No one would dare attack."

Sabin arched a brow. "Do I have to remind you that you and Mel were attacked recently?"

"Not by other princes."

"You don't know that."

"We'll have to find another solution, because I'm not leaving the palace." Berith grinned, and Sabin knew he wouldn't like whatever would come out of his mouth next. "I could send someone I trust."

Sabin stopped to think. Actually, it wasn't such a bad idea, and it was something that had been done before. Sometimes it just wasn't possible for a prince to leave their palace. It could be anything, from their spouse about to give birth to Lucifer ordering them to stay back. It wasn't unheard of for the princes to send someone they trusted on the road for them, and it was something Sabin could work with. He had pity for the poor person who'd be sent out there in Berith's place.

"Fine," he said. "I suppose you can send someone. Who do

you trust enough to do this for you, though?" Sabin could only think of a few people, and none of them would be happy about it.

When Berith didn't answer, Sabin looked at him. Berith was staring, and Sabin stared back until he realized what was happening.

"No," he said. "I'm not doing it."

"There's no one I trust more than you."

"That's a lie. There are plenty of people you trust more than me."

"Not really. There are people I trust as much as I trust you, but not more."

"You could send Aloise."

Berith shook his head. "It wouldn't work. She's not my consort."

"But people know she's the mother of your heir. Surely, it means they'd accept her as your representative."

Berith leaned forward. "She's not going anywhere. You are."

"I can't leave the palace for weeks. I have work to do, and everything will crumble down if I'm not here to make sure people do what they're supposed to do."

"That's why you have assistants. Surely they can hold down the fort until you're back? They would have if you'd left with me."

"You can't order me to go out there in the desert and do this for you."

Berith seemed amused. "Can't I?"

Sabin huffed. "All right, maybe you *can* order me to do it, but you'd never do something like that."

"Not in a normal circumstance, but this is anything but normal. You're right when you say I have to make this trip, but I'm not leaving the palace. That means I need to send someone I trust above everyone else, and that someone is you. You're not my personal assistant because you're my friend,

Sabin. I trust you enough that if something happened to me, I know you'd take care of the palace and my family and that everything would be all right. Besides, you were coming on this trip anyway."

"But I wasn't going to be dealing with the other princes and vassals." That had been Berith's job, and now he wouldn't be there to do it.

There wasn't much Sabin hated more than having to deal with people who wanted something from Berith, but two of those things were traveling and the desert. Unfortunately for him, he'd have to face all three, and while he'd been miserable thinking about it before, now he was pissed.

He pointed his finger at Berith. "This isn't part of my job."

But Berith had decided, and he wouldn't listen to anything Sabin was saying. Sabin could tell from his expression. "You'll do a great job," Berith said as he got to his feet. "And I'll give you plenty of guards to make sure you're safe. You'll be fine, and I'm sure that you'll have done everything you set yourself to do when you come back."

"This is your job, Berith. You can't dump it in my lap just because you want to stay with your consort."

"After what happened recently, I need to stay back to keep an eye on Mel. I'm sure you understand that."

He stared until Sabin started feeling guilty. He didn't want anything to happen to Mel. The human was sweet, and he wasn't used to dealing with demons, even though he'd been living in the palace for months now. He'd always be vulnerable because he was human. Sabin understood that was why Berith wanted to stay, which annoyed him even more. If this had been a tantrum, he would have pushed and yelled at Berith until he agreed to do his job. As it was, he'd feel guilty if he did that.

He glared. "I hate you."

Berith laughed. "You don't. I trust you with my life, Sabin. I know you'll do everything you have to do in order to make sure my territory is safe and that my vassals stay on my side."

"No pressure."

"There's plenty of pressure, but you'll do well. I wouldn't have been able to focus anyway, knowing that Mel could be in trouble."

"You know I hate the desert." Sabin hated everything that wasn't the palace. He liked his comforts, and he didn't want to go out there, trampling in the desert and dealing with people he hated.

But he'd do it. He'd do pretty much anything for Berith, and Berith was very much aware of that. "I'll have that tub you wanted in your bathroom installed while you're gone," he said.

Sabin narrowed his eyes at him. "You think that's going to make me forgive you?"

"In time, hopefully."

"I hate you," Sabin repeated.

"But you also love me."

Berith was right about that, which was why Sabin stopped protesting. He'd already had a lot of work to do before, and now that he knew he'd be going on the road alone, he was panicking. He needed everything to be perfect and ready for when he left. He wouldn't risk his life just to talk to Berith's people.

"If I'm killed, I'll come back and haunt you," he promised.

"And I'll be happy to see you if that's the case."

Sabin was never going to win with Berith, was he? "Whatever. You need to leave. You just dumped a lot of work on my shoulders, and I need to see to it before leaving." Plus, he had to make sure Berith would feel guilty about sending him on this trip on his own.

He'd have to make sure to whine about it every time he was close to Berith. Now *that* sounded fun.

CHAPTER TWO

Sabin looked around, trying to find a reason he couldn't leave. Unfortunately for him, there was nothing, because he'd been the one to organize all of this.

Everything was perfect. The cart where he'd be sitting was as comfortable as possible. The second cart carried enough food and water for him and the guards to be all right until they reached their first stop. A dozen guards would be traveling with him and keeping him safe.

He was ready to go, and he hated it.

"You'll be fine," Berith said from next to him.

Sabin turned to glare at him. "You should hope so. You already know what I'll do if something happens to me."

Berith rolled his eyes. "You'll come back and haunt me. You do realize ghosts aren't real, right?"

"I'll make them real so I can haunt you."

Berith patted Sabin's back with his free hand. His other arm was wrapped around Mel's shoulders, holding him close as everyone watched them saying goodbye to Sabin. Luckily, no one could hear what Sabin was saying except for people who already knew he always talked to Berith that way. Everyone else would have been shocked and angry, and while Sabin didn't care, he didn't want to leave Berith in trouble.

"You'll be fine. Lon chose his best guards to go with you."

Sabin snorted. "That's not true. His best guards are here at the palace with you, Mel, and the rest of your family."

"He chose his second-best guards, then."

Sabin took a deep breath and resisted the urge to hit Berith.

"Whatever. Keep everyone out of trouble."

"I will." Berith's expression softened, and he stepped closer. "Thank you. I know how unhappy you are about doing this and that it's a sacrifice for you. I'm grateful."

Sabin huffed. Why didn't Berith let him cling to his anger? Why did he have to be so nice? "Whatever. I'm not doing it for you."

"No? Who are you doing it for, then?"

"Mel. I like him better than you."

Berith laughed. "I'm sure you do. I'll keep him safe."

"See that you do. I said yes to this stupid thing because I want him to be okay."

Berith was clearly amused, but Mel made a strangled sound and threw his arms around Sabin's neck. Sabin wasn't sure what to make of it or how to react. He hovered his hands over Mel's back, not knowing whether or not he should hug him back, then awkwardly patted him. He looked at Berith, but the asshole was grinning and clearly not about to help Sabin.

"Come home soon," Mel said as he stepped away.

Sabin was relieved the hug was over. "I will. I have no intention of dying just because Berith couldn't get off his ass and do what he needs to do."

Anyone else would be in trouble, but not Sabin. Instead, his words made Berith smile, and he stepped closer. Sabin's eyes went wide when he hugged him, too.

"What are you doing?" he demanded to know.

"Hugging you."

"Why?"

"I don't know. Mel did it."

Sabin pushed him away. "Don't ever hug me again." It wasn't something they did, and it was weird. Sabin could take it from Mel, who was much more emotional and gentler, but from Berith, it was creepy.

"It's time to go," Lon said. He'd been standing next to them the entire time, grinning like an idiot. The smile was gone now, though, and he looked worried.

Sabin sighed. "I'll be careful, and I'll do whatever the guards tell me to do. I promise."

"See that you do. No one wants anything to happen to you."

"I'll be fine. You picked your second-best guards, after all."

That made Lon laugh, but it only lasted for a few seconds. "They'll keep you safe. They're trained, and they know what will happen to them if they allow anyone to hurt you."

"Even if someone does hurt me, I'm sure it won't be their fault." Sabin understood how dangerous this trip was, even with Berith staying back. He wouldn't blame the guards if something happened to him, not when he knew they'd do everything to make sure he was okay. If something happened and any of them managed to come back to the palace, he didn't want them to be punished for something they hadn't been able to stop.

"Come on. I'll help you into the cart," Lon said, offering Sabin his hand.

Sabin took it and climbed in. They'd decided not to take one that was too luxurious so they hopefully would go unnoticed. It would be safer without Berith, and they didn't need it anyway. Sabin supposed he should feel lucky that he wouldn't be forced to walk like the guards would. It made him feel guilty, but he also knew his limitations. If he had to walk, they'd have to stop way too often, and this trip would take ages.

He sat down on the pillows and blankets he'd covered the cart with. He'd be protected from the sun and dust by the curtains that hung all around it, but the heat would be a problem. He supposed he'd have to deal with it.

"Stay safe," Lon said. "I trust these guards with my life."

"Then I suppose I do, too."

"Are you sure he should be doing this?" Sabin heard Mel

ask.

"It's tradition," Berith explained. "The prince or someone he trusts needs to visit the territory every few years."

Sabin glared at him. "It's supposed to be the prince's job," he said loudly.

Berith ignored him. "That way, anyone who can't travel to the palace and has something they want us to know will be able to talk to him."

"All of this would be much easier if you relied more on technology," Mel grumbled. "You have it, so why don't you use it?"

Sabin couldn't say he disagreed, although he knew why they didn't use it. They were lucky here at the palace, where they could buy whatever they needed, but most demons lived in small towns. They couldn't afford anything like technology, which was why he was in this cart right now.

"I'll be fine," he promised Mel.

Mel came closer and squeezed one of Sabin's hands. "I hope so. I don't want to lose you."

"You won't. I have to come back to kill Berith, don't I?"

Mel laughed. "I suppose you do. I'll keep an eye on him until you're back."

"Please do. I have no doubt he'll try to create trouble, but he listens to you."

More than he listened to Sabin, that was for sure.

Sabin wished he could stay here, but eventually, he had to leave. He looked at Lon and nodded, and Lon gave one of the guards the signal they'd been waiting for. The guard moved forward, and the others followed. One of them was guiding the nuckelavee, the horse demons the palace used to pull the carts. When he walked, they followed, and they were off.

Sabin really hoped he'd see the palace again. If he was killed during this mission, he'd fucking kill Berith.

Zeno was better off on his own, but he couldn't always avoid meeting people. He was on his way home, but the food he'd bought was almost gone, which meant he had to stop to get more. He supposed he could hunt something in the desert, but the demons that lived there were nasty, and he walked past towns anyway.

So he'd stopped. He had pulled up his hood, made sure none of his face could be seen, and walked into the town. He was aware of his reputation, and people were afraid enough of him without seeing his face.

Not that there was anything weird about his face. Like almost every other demon, his ancestors were a mix of different species. That meant his face and body were fairly unique, but that was the case for most demons. No, it wasn't his face that had anything wrong.

It was his reputation.

He knew everyone would recognize him if they heard the name he was known by—The Mercenary. He'd become kind of the bogeyman, and while sometimes it made his work easier, other times it was a pain in the ass, like when he needed to buy things. Some people didn't want to serve him, to give him food or anything else, even though he was paying for it. Other people couldn't look away, which was almost as annoying.

Zeno hated being stared at.

Which was what was happening at the moment. When he'd walked into the market, a few demons had noticed him. Once one had realized who he was, though, the word had started spreading. Now, everywhere he turned, people were staring. Usually they quickly looked away when they realized he'd noticed them, only to start again when he turned back.

He stopped at a stall selling bread. The demon behind it swallowed heavily, and when they reached for the bread Zeno pointed at, their hand trembled.

"Give me two of these," Zeno said.

"Right away," the demon squeaked.

Something hit Zeno's leg. He jerked and looked down only to see a little girl losing her balance. He reached out and grabbed her arm, helping her stay on her feet.

"Careful," he grumbled.

She gave him a toothy smile. "You're tall," she said.

Zeno chuckled. "And you're short."

Someone close by sucked in a breath, and Zeno turned to see a female demon rush toward them. She grabbed the little girl's arm and pulled her away, her eyes wide with fear.

The little girl's mother.

She acted as if she expected Zeno to kill the girl just for bumping into him. He realized he had a reputation, but he'd never hurt anyone who hadn't deserved it. When demons tried hiring him to kill someone Zeno deemed innocent, he refused the job. It had never hurt his earnings, and he wasn't about to change that. He wished people realized that, although he supposed it might hurt his reputation.

"Here you go," the demon behind the stall said.

They sounded shaky, and it got even worse when Zeno took the package in which they'd wrapped the bread from their hand. They jerked away as if they expected Zeno to hurt them, and it took a lot for him not to snarl that he wasn't a monster.

Instead of following that instinct, he pushed the package into his bag and took out his money. The demon stared at him, their eyes going wide when he took out a coin.

"You don't need to pay," they said.

Zeno grunted. "Why wouldn't I?"

"You're The Mercenary."

Zeno leaned closer. "I am, but you don't have anything to fear from me." He dropped the coin on the stall. "And my money isn't dangerous or cursed." He wouldn't be surprised if that was why the demon wouldn't take it.

He turned around. He wasn't done with his shopping, and

he wasn't surprised when most of the demons he talked to behaved like the first one. He still managed to buy more food and stuff everything into his bag in the end.

Zeno lived alone, and he stayed home unless he was on a job. He didn't feel lonely, and he liked not having to think of anyone but himself. He didn't need people, and that certainty was reinforced every time he had contact with others. Things would be much easier if he could visit a town, buy what he needed, and get out without people freaking out because of who he was and what they thought they knew about him.

On the one hand, his reputation meant he was left alone, which was what he wanted. On the other, it was annoying when he needed to deal with people.

Since he had everything he needed, he quickly left the small town. He could have found a tavern and gotten a room to rest for a bit, but by now, everyone would know who he was and that he was in town. He'd be better off in the desert. Besides, he preferred walking during the night. It wasn't as hot, which made it easier, even with the predators that came out in the darkness.

He couldn't wait to get home. Hopefully, he wouldn't need to accept another job for a while. The longer he stayed away from other demons, the better it was for his sanity, especially after what had just happened in this tiny little town.

CHAPTER THREE

Sabin flopped back against the pillows in the cart. He sighed deeply, happy to be out of the small town. He realized that not everyone was as lucky as he was, living at the palace, but even though the mayor had offered him a room in her house, it hadn't been what Sabin was used to.

He'd agreed because it would have been rude if he hadn't, but the room had been small and cramped, and it had been evident that the mayor had moved her children to make space for him. It had made Sabin feel guilty, so he was relieved they only had to stay there one night. He'd talked to the mayor over dinner, had written down whatever she wanted to tell Berith, and this morning, they were out. The mayor had tried to convince him to stay for a bit longer, but he'd told her that he had many towns and cities to visit, then he'd rushed out. He was pretty sure his cheek was sticky from something that had been abandoned on the pillow he'd slept on. Hopefully, it was candy.

"Where to this morning?" he asked no one in particular.

The guard walking closest to the cart grunted. "I thought you'd come up with the itinerary?"

Sabin was shocked by the way the guard was talking to him, although maybe he shouldn't be. He was friendly with some of the guards, but he didn't know this one well.

He peered between the curtains. The guard kicked a rock, and Sabin watched as it rolled in front of the cart.

"I was trying to make conversation," he said.

"Of course, sir."

Sabin grimaced. He understood why the guard was calling him that. He was Berith's personal assistant, but that didn't mean he liked being called sir. Also, being on his own with only the guards for company when they barely talked to him wasn't going to make this trip any nicer.

Sabin huffed and closed the curtains. He'd been trying to be friendly, but none of the guards wanted to talk to him any more than the one who just had. It was almost as if they were afraid to say something they shouldn't, which Sabin could understand, but if this was all the interaction they'd have during the entire trip, it was going to be miserable.

He supposed he should have expected it. He'd known the trip wouldn't be great, and that was when he'd been planning on following Berith around. Now he was on his own, and he wasn't sure how to make things better.

Something small whizzed on the other side of the curtain. Sabin glared. The desert had some of the biggest flies he'd ever seen, and he hoped they'd stay outside of the curtain. He already had enough dealing with the dust and heat. The last thing he needed was flies.

"I swear I'm going to strangle Berith as soon as I'm back at the palace," he muttered to himself.

Maybe hearing the sound of his own voice would make him feel less lonely. Loneliness wasn't something he'd expected, and he hadn't planned for it. He wasn't sure he could have. Maybe he should have asked someone he was friends with to come along on this trip, but everyone was busy. His siblings would have been happy to say yes, but just the thought made Sabin shiver in horror. He loved his siblings, but not so much that he wanted to spend days with any of them, stuck in a small cart.

Another whizz caught Sabin's attention. The curtain jerked as if something big had hit it, and something slammed into one of the wooden posts behind him. He turned, wondering if a fly ever had found a way into the cart, only to find an arrow stuck into the wood. He stared at it for a moment, wondering where it had come from. It was still vibrating.

"We're under attack!" one of the guards yelled.

Sabin sucked in a breath. *Right.* That was where the arrow had come from. They were under attack, and someone was apparently trying to kill him.

He pushed away one of the curtains, only to find another arrow coming toward him. He ducked just in time not to be hit.

"Stay inside the cart," the grumpy guard ordered.

Sabin nodded. He wasn't a fighter, and he had no idea what to do in this kind of situation. He'd promised Lon he would obey the guards, and he had every intention of doing so.

Even though it was terrifying.

Screams coming from several people made him look up. His eyes widened at the sight of a group of demons running down the dunes around the cart. A few were carrying bows and arrows, but most had knives and a few even swords. Sabin counted twenty demons, and the number turned his mouth bitter.

There were only twelve guards.

The first scream of pain made him screw his eyes shut. He huddled in the cart, praying the guards would win. What would happen if they didn't?

It was easy to imagine. These demons would either take Sabin for ransom or kill him and take everything of value they could find in the cart. Sabin might be about to die, and there was nothing he could do to save himself.

Something heavy slammed against the side of the cart, making him jump. He sucked in a breath, knowing he had to do something. Yes, he might be about to die, but he wouldn't take it lying down. He might have no idea how to fight, but he could run like everyone else.

He peeked out of the cart. The grumpy guard who'd

ordered him to stay was slumped against the side, his eyes open but unseeing. A knife was embedded in his stomach, and Sabin had to clamp a hand on his mouth to avoid throwing up.

He looked away, but he regretted it as soon as he did. The other guards were in pretty much the same situation as the one against the cart, which didn't bode well. A few were still fighting, but they were outnumbered now, even though they'd managed to kill several of the demons that were attacking them.

Fuck. It didn't look like things were going to be all right.

Sabin had no idea what to do. He wanted to help the guards, but he didn't have a way to do so. Entering the fight would probably make things worse, considering how bad a fighter he was.

But the demons were probably after him. Maybe, if he was gone, they'd leave, too. Maybe they wouldn't, and the guards would be killed, anyway.

The curtain on the other side of the cart was torn away, and Sabin found himself face to face with one of the demons who'd attacked. The demon's horns were high on his forehead, and his nose wasn't unlike a pig's. Sabin wouldn't have known the animal if it wasn't for Cyarea's books, but he clearly remembered reading something about a pig, and the demon in front of him looked like one.

"You're not the prince," the demon grunted.

Sabin shook his head. It made sense. People had to know that Berith's representative was on the road by now. Maybe these demons thought that Berith was here, but they'd been wrong.

Sabin tried to scramble out of the cart, but the demon raised his sword and pressed it against Sabin's throat. Sabin froze, knowing that one little movement would be enough for him to get his throat slashed.

"Who are you?" the demon asked.

Sabin looked around for help, but no one would come. All the guards he'd been traveling with were dead, lying in the sand, their blood soaking into the black dirt. Sabin had no way to know if these demons were going to kill him, but there might be a chance they wouldn't. He just had to be convincing.

He swallowed, and even though the demon didn't move, the blade pressed harder against Sabin's neck.

Right. No swallowing.

"My name is Sabin," he said in a trembling voice.

"I don't care what your name is. I asked you who you are."

"I'm Berith's personal assistant."

The demon grunted yet again. "We want the prince."

"Well, he's not here, but you should keep me alive."

The demon cocked his head. "Should we?"

"You can get a ransom. I'm worth a lot of money to the prince." Or at least, Sabin hoped so.

He and Berith had been friends for a long time, and Berith cared about him, but he'd never negotiated with this kind of demon. When someone was captured, Berith refused to give in, even if it meant that person was killed. Hopefully, Mel would be able to convince him to do something and save Sabin, but Sabin's odds weren't good.

He'd known this trip was a mistake, dammit.

Everything looked the same in the desert. It was quite boring, but it was also soothing in a way. Apart from animals, Zeno didn't have to worry about anyone attacking him. He'd be home tomorrow if he continued walking as fast as he was, and he couldn't wait.

The sound of two swords clashing made him freeze. It was out of place, but he'd recognize it anywhere. Someone was fighting nearby, and from the sound of it, they were trying to kill each other.

Zeno hesitated. It was none of his business, and he should stay away from whatever was happening. No one had paid him to intervene, and staying out of other people's business was something he prided himself on.

Still, he continued walking. The sounds of the fight became louder, but he tried to ignore them. He skirted away from the fight, keeping a good distance from the sounds he could hear. Demons were dying, but demons died every day, and once again, it was none of his business.

Then he heard the voice.

"He'll give you a lot of money for me," it said.

"How do I know I can believe you?" another asked. It was deeper, close to a grunt.

"How do I know I can trust you not to kill me anyway?"

Voice one wasn't wrong. Zeno wasn't sure who these demons were, but there were several bands of them in this area. They attacked travelers, trying to get as many goods and coins as they could. Usually they killed everyone they found, but it seemed they hadn't today. It made him wonder who they'd caught, and he decided that peeking down the dune wouldn't be too much of a problem. He wasn't going to step in, merely to see what was happening. He pitied whoever had been attacked, but it wasn't his job to save them.

He climbed the closest dune, intent on peeking around to make sure it wasn't anyone he knew. He'd leave if it wasn't. He wasn't sure what to expect when he reached the top of the dune, but it wouldn't be the first time he saw travelers being attacked.

Sure enough, there were bodies down there. He'd expected that, so he wasn't surprised. He hadn't expected to see that most of the bodies wore some kind of uniform. Whoever was traveling had clearly hired them to protect them, but the guards hadn't done a good job. Zeno was sure they'd been well-trained, but the demons who lived and hunted around here were feral. These guards probably hadn't known what hit them.

Zeno's gaze drifted over to the cart. There were two of them, but it seemed like all of the demons who'd attacked were gathered around one. He cocked his head, trying to see what they were doing. He counted a dozen demons, with more dead in the sand. The guards might all have died, but they hadn't gone alone.

One of the demons gathered around the cart stepped aside, and Zeno finally saw the person they were talking to. He was huddled in the cart, looking terrified, yet he kept his chin high, and he was talking as if he didn't have a care in the world. Anyone with eyes could see that he was scared, but Zeno was still impressed. It took a lot to stand up to these demons, especially when one wasn't a fighter.

The demon was an onah demon, and from his looks, he was pretty pure. His hair was a deep purple, just like the tail Zeno could see wrapped around his waist. Two short black horns shot out of his head, and his pointed ears were long and lined with earrings. He looked out of place, but then Zeno supposed he wouldn't be sticking around. Once these demons had whatever they wanted, they'd kill him.

Zeno wasn't sure why this made him feel sad.

"How much will he give us?" one of the demons who'd attacked said with a grunt.

"Anything you want. I'm one of his closest friends."

One of the other demons laughed. "You, the friend of the prince?"

The onah looked offended. He straightened his back, but nothing could change the fact that he was sitting in the cart. "I'll have you know that I've worked for him for years. I know him better than most people, and yes, he'll pay a lot to get me back."

That gave Zeno one more reason to step in, although he still didn't understand why he wanted to do so. He had more than enough money to go on for several months without having to take a job. He didn't need more money, yet it tempted him.

Almost as much as he wanted the demon in the cart.

Zeno didn't often have that kind of impulse. He was better off on his own, and even when he decided it was time to scratch the itch and have sex, it was always anonymous. He chose someone in the closest town, fucked them in an alley, and went home.

He wouldn't be able to do that with the onah demon. Even if the demon was lying about whatever prince of Hell he supposedly was friends with, he looked completely out of place in the desert. He was delicate looking, and it was clear he didn't belong. He was nothing like the people Zeno had sex with, so that was probably out. It would be for the best, anyway, just in case Zeno had to kill him.

But if he didn't kill him, he stood to get a lot of money. He wouldn't even have to ransom this demon. Maybe it would be enough for him to take the onah home, and he'd be so grateful he'd pay Zeno.

Zeno shook his head. He didn't want any complications, and the onah demon had complications written all over him.

Zeno turned to leave, but a cry made him stop again.

"What are you doing?" the onah demon asked.

"Making sure you don't have weapons hidden on your body," one of the other demons said.

His friends laughed, and Zeno had a pretty good idea of what the demon was doing. For some reason, it made him see red.

He was used to living in the desert. He knew how hard it was, how cruel the people who lived here had to be. He'd always tried not to become like them, but he wasn't sure he'd succeeded, at least not entirely. If there was one thing he'd never done, though, it was hurting demons who didn't deserve it. He'd drawn a line there long ago, and he always respected it.

The same couldn't be said for these demons.

They'd attacked travelers, and while Zeno suspected they would keep the onah demon alive for ransom, it didn't mean they wouldn't hurt him. For some reason, that was unacceptable for Zeno.

He sighed. He was going to get involved, and he wasn't even sure why.

He dropped his bag in the sand, creating a small cloud of dust. He cracked his neck this way and that, made sure his hood was firmly in place, and took a step toward the cart.

He wasn't surprised to see the onah demon had been dragged out of it. He was pressed against one side of the cart, clearly torn between moving closer to the body of the guard sitting there just to be away from the demons who'd attacked and staying closer to the demons surrounding him. One of the demons reached for him, catching his arm and pulling him up. The onah demon cried out again, and that gave Zeno the last push he needed to step in.

He made his way down the dune.

It took a moment for any of the demons to notice him. They were too focused on the onah demon. As soon as Zeno killed the first, the others turned to face him. They gaped at him, clearly not having expected anyone to attack them, but he could see the moment they decided he didn't matter. He was alone, after all, while there were thirteen of them—twelve now that he'd killed one.

Not a problem. Zeno had killed more demons at once.

"What are you waiting for?" the demon holding the onah demon said. "Kill him."

Eleven demons ran at Zeno. A few appeared terrified, maybe because they recognized him. Others didn't seem to know who he was, and they threw themselves at him, raising their weapons. Zeno already had his sword in his hands, and he slashed into whatever demon came too close. He couldn't say he enjoyed killing, but he also couldn't have cared less about what happened to these demons. As far as he was concerned, they were attacking him, which meant they deserved to be killed.

And they'd get exactly that.

Sabin had no idea who this new demon was, but they were killing the demons who'd attacked him, so they had to be good.

Right?

He watched in awe and horror as the new demon mowed through the ones who threw themselves at him. They'd obeyed the order of the demon who was still holding Sabin's arm so hard that Sabin wondered if he might break it. It certainly felt like he might, and trying to pull out of his hold had only made him tighten it.

A head rolled in Sabin's direction, and he scrambled to get away from it. The eyes of the demon it belonged to seemed to stare through him, giving him the creeps. He wasn't entirely sure why he wasn't afraid of the demon killing the others, but maybe it was because the enemy of his enemy was his friend, or something like that. If this demon freed Sabin, Sabin would make sure he was rewarded handsomely for it. He'd rather pay this demon than pay the ones who'd attacked him and had killed all the guards.

Sabin was a demon, and he'd always lived in Hell. He knew he was sheltered, and he'd never seen so much blood and pain. He screwed his eyes shut, but even so, he was pretty sure he'd see the images etched into the back of his eyelids for the rest of his life. He could smell blood and screams filled the air, along with other sounds that turned his stomach.

The demon holding Sabin let him go. It startled Sabin so much that he blinked his eyes open, wondering what the demon was doing. He expected him to be attacking the new demon, but instead, the asshole was running the other way. He hadn't even stolen anything. He was running, and when

Sabin turned to look at his friends, he understood why.

All of them were dead.

Sabin twisted his torso to throw up to the side, only to come face to face with the dead guard. He scrambled away, but he had nowhere to go. He supposed he could run away like the last demon was, but where would he go? He didn't know the desert. He'd get lost here just as easily as he could get killed, and then, what would he do? His only hope was the demon who'd killed the ones who'd attacked, so he sucked in a breath, kept his breakfast in his stomach, and turned to look at them.

The demon was staring at the one running away. Sabin couldn't see their face because they were wearing a hood, but he could see the four horns poking from under it. Two of them curled around the demon's face to frame it, while the others went upward toward the sky. They were as black as the night and the sand under Sabin.

The demon's shoulders slumped, and he pulled his arm back. For a moment, Sabin wondered what he was doing. Then the demon jerked his hand forward, and a knife flew from it.

Sabin held his breath as he watched the knife fly. He expected it to fall to the ground eventually, but instead, it reached the demon running away. Sabin was stunned because the demon was so distant, but the knife embedded into the demon's back, and the demon cried out and fell to the ground.

Then there was silence.

Sabin didn't think he'd ever experienced such a deep silence. He couldn't hear anything except for the sound of his own breath. It was too fast and erratic, but who would have blamed him, considering the situation? He'd been saved from the demons who'd attacked him and who'd killed all the guards, but what about this new demon?

They hadn't even looked at Sabin yet. They were walking toward the last demon, possibly to retrieve their knife. It gave

Sabin the opportunity to run away, and he got to his hooves, his legs trembling under him. He had to cling to the cart so he wouldn't fall on his face, which didn't bode well for him running away.

Besides, even if he did run, the desert would kill him. He had no idea where to go, how to survive here, or how to go home. No, his only hope was the demon who'd saved him, and he watched as they leaned toward the body on the ground. He was pretty sure he saw the demon they'd hit with the knife crawl forward, but after his savior leaned even closer and did something, he stopped moving.

Then the new demon turned toward Sabin.

Sabin swallowed. He'd offer this demon the same thing he'd offered the others. He needed help, and this was the only demon around. Sabin would have to trust him, no matter how hard that sounded.

He was surprised when the demon didn't make a beeline for him. Instead, they headed in the direction from which they'd come from, barely looking at Sabin. Sabin saw them lean forward again, pick up a bag, and haul it onto their shoulder. Then they turned around and started walking away.

Were they leaving Sabin alone in the desert?

Sabin rushed forward. He almost fell, tripping on the feet of the guard who'd been killed next to the cart. He did his best to ignore it, but he realized he wouldn't be able to keep up with this demon. "Wait!" he yelled.

Luckily for him, the demon stopped moving. However, they didn't turn, which Sabin suspected was a sign they'd leave if they didn't like what he was about to say.

He wasn't sure what to offer. The easiest would be money like he had for the other demons, but that would imply he was a prisoner. He prayed that whatever the reason the demon had killed the others that it was to save him, which meant this demon wouldn't want to imprison him.

"I need you to take me home," he said.

The demon's shoulders tightened. "I can't."

The voice was male, or at least, Sabin thought so. He took another step forward, proud when his knees didn't give up under him. "Why not? I'll pay you as much as you want."

The demon finally turned around. "How much are we talking?"

Sabin didn't know how much money would be enough for this guy. He didn't want to offer too much, but he also didn't want to offer too little. He was sure that if he didn't have enough money to pay this demon himself, Berith would pitch in. He owed it to Sabin after sending him out on his own, dammit.

"Whatever you want. If you want gold, I'll give it to you. If you want a home, a business, or something else, I'll make sure you get them."

The demon cocked his head. Sabin still couldn't see his expression — it was creepy knowing he was being watched without being able to see who it was. He stayed where he was, standing as tall as he could, hoping that whatever the demon was seeing would make him say yes.

But instead, the demon shook his head and turned around again.

"Wait!" Sabin said. "What are you doing? I told you I'd pay you."

"I don't need money."

"It doesn't have to be money. It can be whatever you want."

"I don't need anything."

The demon was far enough away that he had to yell for Sabin to be able to hear him. Soon he'd be so far that Sabin wouldn't be able to see him, and he'd be left alone.

Sabin disliked being alone.

He'd never been alone in his life. Onah demons lived in big family clans, so before moving into his rooms at the palace, he lived with both his mothers, his grandmother, his uncle, and his six siblings. Even now that he had his own rooms in the palace, he was with others all the time. The only times he was alone were at night, and since he was asleep, it didn't matter.

But here, the loneliness was already weighing on his shoulders. The desert was so vast that it freaked him out, and he wouldn't be able to navigate it on his own. He had no idea where to go, but the best thing would be to go back to the palace. It was several days behind him, though, and it would be too easy for him to get lost.

So he did the only thing he could do. He took a shaky step, then another, and went after his savior. Hopefully, the demon wouldn't decide to kill him because he was annoying him. Even if he did, at least Sabin wouldn't die alone.

CHAPTER FOUR

Zeno felt just a bit guilty about abandoning the demon in the desert. He told himself that he'd already saved the demon's life, after all. He didn't need to take the demon home, too. Surely if the demon was in the desert, he'd know how to get out of it.

But Zeno could hear the demon scrambling to come after him. Having the demon follow him would spell trouble, but there wasn't anything Zeno could do beyond killing him.

"What are you doing?" he asked with a growl.

His tone wasn't enough to stop the demon from following him. "I'm coming with you."

"Who said you could?"

The demon had barely started walking, yet, he was already out of breath. "What else am I supposed to do?" he panted. "If I stay here on my own, I'll die."

"And why should I care about that?"

"Maybe you don't, but I suspect you do."

"Why?"

"Because you wouldn't have saved me from those demons if you didn't care at least a bit."

He had Zeno there. Zeno still didn't understand why he'd stepped in and saved the onah demon, but he had. Wasn't it his responsibility to make sure the demon made it out of the desert alive?

It wasn't. Zeno hadn't wanted the demon to die, but he would if he didn't step in. What was Zeno supposed to do? He didn't work with people. He barely *talked* to people, and he was honestly surprised that the onah demon wasn't afraid of him. He'd seen him kill thirteen demons without hesitation.

"My name is Sabin," the onah demon said.

"Aren't you afraid I'm going to kill you?"

"I suppose you could. Why didn't you, after you killed all those other demons?"

Sabin was struggling to keep up with Zeno, and Zeno found himself going more slowly. What the fuck was he doing?

"We should probably go back to the carts," Sabin said.

"We won't use the carts. I only travel by foot," Zeno snapped at him.

"I didn't say anything about using the carts, but we could free the nuckelavee and grab some of the food and water."

That gave Zeno pause. Sabin wasn't wrong, and while Zeno had enough food and water to last him until he got home, it wouldn't be nearly enough for Sabin. Zeno had saved him from those demons. He felt responsible for him and for getting him out of the desert.

He stopped walking. Sabin was still scrambling to reach him, but he was panting and sweating. He had nothing to cover his head and protect himself from the sun, which was stupid.

Sabin pressed his hands to his knees and leaned down as he tried to get his breath back. "Good. You stopped. I knew you would."

"Did you?" Zeno suspected Sabin hadn't recognized him as The Mercenary. Otherwise he'd have run the other way screaming. Instead, he was acting as if Zeno was his new best friend, which Zeno supposed was right. Sabin wouldn't make it out of the desert alone, and Zeno was the only person around.

"You wouldn't have saved me from those demons if you didn't want me to live, and you know I'll die if I'm left on my own in the desert," Sabin said. He straightened and looked at

Zeno.

He was even prettier from up close. Most demons were mixed breeds, but if there was something more than onah in Sabin, Zeno couldn't see it. Sabin's long purple hair curled around his face and all the way down in front of his chest, and his tail swiped behind him, raising small clouds of dust. The tail started behind Sabin and curled around his legs as if it had a life of its own. It thinned down its length, and the tip had two fins of delicate skin. It looked a bit like a fish's tail, but much prettier.

Even the hair on Sabin's leg, dark purple like on his head, was attractive. Zeno didn't mind the hooves, either. They would certainly make the walk in the desert easier on Sabin.

Sabin's lower body, from his waist down, was covered in dark purple fur. He wore a white gown thing, but it was almost transparent. It concealed all the bits Sabin didn't want people to see, but Zeno found himself imagining them, anyway.

Sabin's upper body looked like a human's. He had black claws, but his skin was pale, and it was already starting to turn red from the sun. Zeno could even see dark purple freckles appearing on his nose and cheeks.

No one should be so adorable. Sticking with Sabin was the stupidest idea Zeno ever had, but he still found himself wanting to make sure the onah demon was okay. He didn't hurt demons who didn't deserve it, and if he abandoned Sabin, Sabin would get hurt. It would be Zeno's fault, and Zeno couldn't allow that to happen.

Sabin put his hands on his hips. "Why are you staring?"

"How do you know I'm staring?" Zeno was still wearing his hood, so Sabin couldn't see him.

"I can feel it. Why do you wear that hood?"

"Maybe I'm too ugly for anyone to see me."

Sabin snorted. "I doubt that's the case." He tilted his head up. "It protects you from the sun."

Zeno sighed. If he was going to take Sabin home, they'd need some of the supplies from the carts.

Zeno walked past Sabin, having decided that the best thing he could do was be quick. The many bodies he'd left on the sand would soon attract predators, and it wouldn't be good for him and Sabin to still be here when it happened.

Sabin scrambled to keep up with him. "I told you my name, but I don't know yours," he pointed out.

"Why do you care?"

"I don't." Sabin sounded almost happy. "I can continue calling you my savior."

Zeno grimaced. He wasn't anyone's savior, and he didn't want anyone to call him that. "I'm Zeno."

Sabin hummed. He sounded way too happy, considering what had just happened to him. "I like that name. It's strong, short, and to the point, very much like you."

Zeno was glad Sabin couldn't see him, because he was smiling under his hood. "You don't know anything about me."

"I know enough to know you're strong and that you get straight to the point. I've watched you fight, remember?"

How could Zeno not remember?

He and Sabin had reached the carts, and the proof of what Zeno had done was spread out all around them.

He went straight for the second cart, the one without the curtains in which Sabin had been sitting when he'd first seen him. Sabin followed him, his hooves making no noise on the sand.

"The guards you hired weren't that great," he said with a grunt.

"Yeah, well, the best guards had to stay back at the palace. Their job is to protect the prince, not me."

That gave Zeno pause. He hadn't thought Sabin was telling the truth when he'd said he was friends with a prince of Hell, but what reason would he have to lie now? "You're really friends with a prince of Hell?" he asked.

He started looking through things in the cart, putting aside some of the food. They shouldn't take too much because they had to carry it, and he was glad to find a bag. Sabin would need to carry some of the stuff, too. Hopefully he wouldn't be prissy about it.

"I'm his personal assistant. We've been friends for years, and I wasn't lying when I said that he'd pay you handsomely for taking me home."

"I wasn't lying when I told you I didn't need money."

Sabin huffed. Zeno was amused when he saw that Sabin was glaring at him, but he kept his amusement to himself.

"He'll give you whatever you want. If you want a palace, done. It's yours. You want a title? We have plenty of those to give around."

Zeno shook his head. He didn't know what he wanted, but he suspected that the demon standing next to him was one of those things.

Which meant he was in trouble.

Sabin still wasn't sure what to make of Zeno. The demon was fierce, strong, and didn't hesitate to kill, but he was also kind of nice. Sabin hoped he'd convinced him not to kill him in his sleep and take him home, but he couldn't tell. The fact that he couldn't see Zeno's face didn't make it any easier.

He didn't think Zeno hid his face because he was ugly like Zeno had said. Something niggled at the back of his mind, something he felt he should recognize, but he couldn't quite pin it down. It would come to him when he wasn't thinking about it, so he didn't try to force himself to.

Zeno turned toward him and handed him something. Sabin took it without thinking, and he found himself with an armful of bag containing food and water.

He sighed. He'd known he would have to pull his weight

if Zeno agreed to take him home, and he had every intention of doing so, but he wasn't looking forward to the next few days. Hell, he wasn't even sure how long it would take him to get back to the palace. Would it be days or weeks? They wouldn't be using the carts, which meant they were going on foot. Sabin wasn't the strongest walker, unfortunately.

"Which prince?" Zeno asked.

Sabin hesitated. He didn't know Zeno, but he had to trust him. Otherwise, he'd die before reaching the palace. "Berith."

Zeno froze for just a second. Then he started moving again, poking through the things in the cart. "He's powerful," he said.

"He is, and he's rich. You believe me, then?"

"I don't see why you'd lie to me."

"So you do believe I'm Berith's personal assistant." Why did it sound like Sabin was trying to convince Zeno that he wasn't? He needed to stop that.

"Yes."

"And you'll take me home?"

Zeno grunted. "I already told you I would. Now shut up and grab as much food as you can. We need to get out of here."

There was an urgency in Zeno's tone that told Sabin he had a good reason for wanting them to leave. He was too afraid to ask, so he kept his mouth shut and obeyed Zeno's order.

By the time they were done, the bag was heavy, and Sabin was a little afraid because he'd have to carry it all the way back to the palace. It was either that or die from hunger or thirst, and he wasn't about to find out how that felt. So he hauled the bag onto his shoulder and looked at Zeno expectantly.

The hood thing was going to become old, fast.

"Can't you take that thing down?" he asked, gesturing at Zeno's face.

"Why would I?"

"Because I want to see your face. You've seen mine."

"So has the sun. You're burning."

Sabin grimaced and gingerly touched his cheek. "I'm very much aware of that. There's not much I can do, though."

Zeno looked around, then walked away from Sabin. Sabin scrambled to go after him, but he didn't go far. He stopped at the first cart, grabbed one of the curtains, and pulled.

The sound of tearing fabric was loud in the silence of the desert. Sabin watched as Zeno finished tearing down the curtain, then brought it to Sabin. He held his breath, but the only thing Zeno did was wrap it around Sabin's face and head. It was hot, but it gave him a little shade, which was what he needed.

Sabin reached up and clutched the edge of the curtain. "Thank you."

Zeno grunted. "You're welcome. Can we go now?"

"Of course. Why are you so much in a rush, though?"

"It's a miracle the predators aren't here to eat the dead yet."

Sabin gasped. "They're going to be eaten?" He hadn't allowed himself to think about what would happen to the bodies of the guards who'd defended him. They'd done their job as well as they could, but they'd died anyway. It made Sabin feel guilty that he was still alive, but he pushed that thought away. He'd been lucky, and no one would berate him for that. Besides, if Zeno hadn't stepped in when he had, Sabin suspected that while he would be alive, he would wish he weren't.

"That's how things work in the desert," Zeno said as he started walking away.

Sabin had to go after him, but first he went around both carts to free the nuckelavee. He didn't know what would happen to them or if they could survive on their own in the desert, but at least like this, they'd have a chance.

Once he was done, he rushed after Zeno. The other demon hadn't waited for him, but he wasn't walking as fast as the first time Sabin ran after him. He was acting as if he didn't care whether or not Sabin followed him, but it was obvious that he actually did. He wouldn't have been walking so slowly otherwise.

"So, what will you ask from Berith?" Sabin asked. He could feel Zeno's gaze on him, even though he couldn't see it.

"Gold, probably."

"No palace?"

"I don't need a palace. I already have a home."

"Where is it?"

"None of your business."

Sabin was disappointed but not surprised. Zeno seemed like the kind of demon who kept his life private to the extreme. On the other hand, Sabin had already told him that he and Berith were best friends.

Maybe he should start watching what he said. It was probably too late, but still.

Talking had always made Sabin feel better. He wasn't afraid of Zeno, exactly, but he was wary. He didn't know what to make of the other demon, and Zeno wasn't making things easier on him. Maybe if Zeno told Sabin about his life, Sabin would relax and stop being afraid, but instead, Zeno was utterly silent as they walked.

"You'll take me home, right?" Sabin asked eventually.

"Where did you think I was taking you?" Zeno sounded amused.

"I don't know. Maybe to your home to kill and eat me."

"Not enough meat on you."

It took Sabin a second to realize Zeno was teasing him. "I don't know. I think there *is* a little meat on me." Sabin patted his stomach. It was exposed to the warm air, but with the curtain still wrapped around his shoulders and head, it wouldn't burn.

Probably.

Zeno twisted his neck to look at Sabin. Sabin could have

sworn he was looking him up and down, so he wasn't surprised when Zeno grunted and said, "Looks good to me."

That shouldn't have pleased Sabin as much as it did.

"I suppose it comes with the territory," he explained. "I've been living at the palace for years now, and the food the cooks come up with is incredible. You wouldn't believe it if I told you about it."

"You live a luxurious life."

"I'm sure it's nothing like yours. If it weren't for you, I'd probably be dead already."

"They wouldn't have killed you after you told them about your friend."

But there were worse things than death.

Sabin understood how lucky he'd been that Zeno had been walking past and that he'd stopped to help. Many demons wouldn't have. Sabin wouldn't have blamed them for it, but he was glad Zeno had helped him.

Zeno knew how to wield his weapons and had experience killing demons. It made Sabin curious, but while he wanted to ask Zeno what he did for a living, he didn't dare. He didn't want to do anything that would push Zeno to abandon him in the middle of the desert.

Still, he would have felt better if he'd known more about the other demon. He didn't know how long it would take them to reach the palace, but it looked like they had at least a few days—if not more—of walking ahead of them.

That would give him more than enough time to poke and prod at Zeno and find out more about him, his life, and why he'd stopped to help Sabin.

CHAPTER FIVE

"I hate the desert. I hate the heat. I hate all of this." Sabin kicked a rock, sending it skittering in front of him. He pulled up the bag he was carrying higher on his shoulder, but the damn thing slid down again. Sabin had to resist the urge to throw it in the sand and scream.

Zeno was just ahead of him, silent. He hadn't said much since they'd started walking, and Sabin was starting to realize he was a demon of few words. He also still hadn't taken down his hood, which made Sabin desperately curious to see what his face looked like. He'd started imagining it, if anything, to distract himself from how much he hated the desert, but it was impossible to guess.

Where to start? Zeno had four horns, which was unusual but not unseen. Most demons had horns, so there was no way to guess what kind of demon he could be. He was probably a mix, like most demons. The horns were black, which didn't help, even with one missing its tip. Sabin could think of one kind of demon that had four black horns, so maybe Zeno was an agramon demon? It would explain why Zeno's shoulders appeared so massive under the garment he used to cover most of his body. If Sabin squinted, he thought he could see some of the spikes agramon demons had on parts of their body. They were similar to the horns but much smaller.

Sabin cocked his head. What else could he see? Zeno's body seemed to be similar to a human's, with two legs, two arms, and one head. He didn't have hooves like Sabin, and he was wearing shoes. Sabin had seen his hands, but unfortunately, he hadn't paid much attention at the time. He remembered a flash of gray, so maybe Zeno's skin was gray? Ghouls were gray, but that didn't seem to be Zeno's species, because he didn't smell of death.

Just the thought made Sabin shudder in horror. Ghouls were nasty from every point of view, including a demon's.

"I can feel you staring," Zeno suddenly said.

Sabin stumbled and almost fell. One of Zeno's arms shot back, grabbing Sabin before he could faceplant. Sabin grabbed the arm, and his fingers slid under the long-sleeved tunic Zeno was wearing.

Zeno's skin was smooth but bumpy in some places. Sabin looked down, curious and not one bit surprised to see a big hand tipped with black claws. He had black claws, too.

He'd been right. Zeno's skin was gray — not the deadly gray of ghouls, but rather a light gray that Sabin wanted to see more of.

"Sabin?" Zeno asked.

Sabin realized he was staring again, and even worse, this time, he was holding on to Zeno. He snatched his hands away and looked up at the other demon, forcing a smile on his lips. "I'm fine. Once again, you saved me."

Zeno snorted. "From what? The sand?"

"Falling face first on it wouldn't have been pleasant."

"I suppose it wouldn't have. You're up to continue walking for a bit longer?"

Sabin wanted to say no, slump onto the sand, and stay there forever, but instead, he nodded. Zeno was saving his life, taking him away from the desert, and Sabin didn't want to bother him any more than he already had. Wasting time would piss him off, and besides, he wanted to get back to the palace. He needed a bath and to be away from all this dust and heat.

The curtain that was still wrapped around his head and shoulders protected him from the sun, but it also made him feel hot. He wanted to tear it off and scream, but that would attract whatever predator was hiding under the sand, and besides, Sabin didn't want to act like an idiot. It would be too easy to send Zeno running, and then, what would Sabin do? He'd be alone in the middle of the desert, and he wouldn't know which way to go. He'd completely lost his orientation, and he had no idea if they were going in the direction of the palace or somewhere else. As far as he knew, Zeno might be kidnapping him and planning on killing him to eat him, like he'd teased before.

He shook his head and started following Zeno again. Zeno wasn't going to hurt him. He'd had plenty of time to do so since they'd started walking, but instead, he was taking care of him. He was the only person Sabin could trust at the moment, and Sabin needed that.

He also needed to break the silence that made all of this even creepier than it already was.

"So you know what kind of demon I am," he said.

Zeno grunted. "Onah."

"Yep. Both my parents are, as is my second mother. I guess it's kind of obvious."

Zeno grunted again. He was staring ahead, and Sabin couldn't tell if he was annoyed at the stream of words coming out of his mouth. He supposed Zeno would tell him if that was the case.

"But I'm not sure what kind of demon *you* are. I mean, it's pretty much impossible to guess, since you haven't shown me your face. Do you think you're going to eventually? Are we going to stay the entire time in the desert, or will we stop in some towns or something? I know we have enough food and water to last us for a while, but I have no idea where we are. How long will it take us to get back to the palace?"

"Do you ever shut up?" Zeno asked.

There was no heat in his voice, which reassured Sabin. He didn't want to annoy Zeno any more than he already had, but if he didn't fill the silence, he was going to scream. "Not really. If you want to be heard in my family, you have to speak up. There are seven kids, including me, and of course, my mothers, my grandmother, and my uncle."

"Onah demons live in clans."

Sabin beamed. He wasn't sure why, but it was nice that Zeno knew something about him.

It would be nicer if *he* knew something about *Zeno*.

"We do! I'm the weird one because I left home, but everyone else still lives together."

"Why would it be weird?"

"Because we continue living in our clan until we're ready to start our own family, usually. Then we become a new clan. I haven't done that, though. I left the clan and moved into the palace, but I don't have a family." Sabin snorted softly. "I don't have anyone, really."

Zeno was silent for a moment, and Sabin thought he'd finally annoyed him so much that he wasn't going to answer. He wouldn't be surprised. He was blathering, and it was clear that Zeno was a demon of few words.

"Why did you leave your clan?" Zeno asked after a moment.

Sabin was more than happy to talk about anything, including his private life. "Why not?"

"I wouldn't be asking you if I knew."

"No, I get that. What I meant was that I didn't *have* to stay with the clan. Yes, it's what we usually do, but we don't actually have to do it."

"And you didn't want to?"

"I love my family, and I visit often, but it's impossible to have something of your own with six siblings. I guess I wanted people to see me for who I was, not because I was part of the clan."

Zeno grunted, maybe because he understood, maybe because he didn't and wanted Sabin to shut up. Sabin had no way to know. Until Zeno told him to stop talking, he wasn't going to.

"I was lucky that Berith gave me a chance."

"How did you become a prince of Hell's friend?"

"Oh, he wasn't a prince of Hell when we first met. He was an asshole, although I suppose he still is most of the time. Meeting Mel helped, but the poor guy can't work miracles."

"Mel?"

"Berith's consort? I thought everyone had heard about him by now. I mean, he's not only Berith's consort, but he's also human." Sabin wasn't telling Zeno anything every single demon in Berith's territory wasn't aware of already.

"A prince of Hell took a human as consort?"

Sabin was pretty sure he could hear the surprise in Zeno's tone. "Yes. Have you been living under a rock? I'm pretty sure every single demon in Hell knows about him by now, and probably most demons in the human realm, too."

Zeno grunted again. Sabin doubted he'd get a different answer, but he didn't need one. He was fine talking as if he were on his own.

Which was what he continued doing.

Zeno hadn't known someone could talk as much as Sabin was. He'd never met anyone who was so vocal, and he wasn't sure what to do about it, or even if there was anything he should do. Sabin's voice might attract predators, but Zeno couldn't find it in himself to tell him to shut up. He could tell Sabin was talking so much because he was nervous and afraid, and if it helped him settle down, Zeno was all for it.

He also kind of liked it.

He wasn't sure why, and that annoyed him. He was used to being on his own. He barely spoke, and people certainly didn't speak to him. They didn't tell him about their family, and they didn't ask him questions about himself. Sabin had, a few times, but Zeno hadn't answered any of them.

He wasn't sure he could.

Zeno had no idea what to do with someone who wanted to get to know him. He would've thought they'd been paid to find his weaknesses if it had been anyone else. No one had ever tried that, but it wouldn't be a surprise. He was *The Mercenary*, and some demons wanted nothing more than to kill him. One of the reasons he'd survived all these years was by not caring about anyone, not having a family or someone he loved. Clearly, the same couldn't be said for Sabin.

Sabin had an entire clan of onah demons who loved him. He didn't realize how lucky he was, but Zeno wasn't about to bring that up. It wasn't Sabin's fault that Zeno was on his own.

"Anyway, Mel is delightful," Sabin continued, bringing Zeno's mind back to the fact that a prince of Hell had taken a human as his consort.

When had that happened, and how did it work? Zeno knew of humans who lived in Hell, so he was aware of the fact that some spells could be used to make sure they survived, but all the humans he'd seen here were slaves. He'd never heard about a demon being in love with a human, and he'd certainly never heard about a prince of Hell making one of them his consort.

It might explain why Sabin was in the desert on his own. Zeno hadn't asked what Sabin had been doing there, but maybe he'd been traveling for the prince. If the prince had a human in his bed, it made sense he wouldn't want to leave the palace. It would leave the human vulnerable, and one of the prince's enemies might try to kill him.

Zeno wanted to know more about the human, but he wasn't about to ask, either. Maybe if he let Sabin run his mouth, he'd find out more about Sabin's life, including the consort.

"He had no idea what to do when he first arrived, you

know?" Sabin said.

Zeno didn't know, so he listened.

"He was terrified of us, and I don't blame him. He was taken from the human realm because one of Berith's enemies was trying to make Berith look bad. He thought Berith would kill Mel or something like that, but instead, Berith treated him well. They even fell in love, which wasn't something I ever expected to happen. Berith isn't exactly the kind of demon who falls in love." Sabin snorted. "I suppose he is, actually. He's been different since Mel entered his life. He's still the same old prince of Hell, but there's a softness to him that wasn't there before."

Zeno couldn't imagine that a prince of Hell being soft was a good thing.

"But that doesn't mean he's a bad prince," Sabin quickly added, as if he could read Zeno's mind. "That was one of the problems with Mel in the beginning, and still a bit now. He had to get used to how demons live, and that included violence. I mean, he's a teacher. When he was in the human realm, he worked with kids. He didn't deal with any kind of violence, so it was a big change."

Sabin was so focused on what he was saying that he wasn't looking where he was going. He stumbled, and Zeno had to reach for him. He'd been doing that again and again, and he wondered if Sabin even realized that he'd come to rely on him. Probably not. He was too focused on telling Zeno about this Mel, himself, and whatever else crossed his mind, and every time he stumbled, he accepted Zeno's help, steadied himself, and continued walking—and talking.

Zeno was surprised Sabin hadn't stopped to throw a tantrum yet. He'd been bitching that he hated the desert, the heat, and everything else, and Zeno couldn't say he disagreed. He was used to living here, but that didn't mean he liked it. Sabin was vocal enough for both of them, so Zeno had kept his mouth shut.

He slowed down just a bit so Sabin would walk ahead of him. He eyed the onah demon, but no matter how many times he tried to understand him, he couldn't.

Sabin was a palace boy. Even now that he was sweaty and dirty, it was obvious. He was used to his comforts, and in the desert, there were none. Zeno wouldn't have been surprised if Sabin demanded he carry him or if he stopped in the middle of the desert, sat down, and refused to take one more step. It was clear Sabin wasn't used to walking so much, yet he kept on. He was complaining plenty, but he continued putting one hoof in front of the other. Zeno was impressed, because not many demons would have done so. The desert was hard on everyone, including him, but Sabin was keeping up. Zeno had slowed down considerably, and he made sure to stop more often than he would if he'd been alone, but still. None of that changed the fact that Sabin had an inner strength Zeno hadn't expected.

Sabin was nothing like Zeno had expected, and he didn't know what to do with the demon. Well, he'd take Sabin home, but he was surprised to realize that he'd miss Sabin once they parted ways. That didn't make sense, but Zeno tried not to hide from himself.

Maybe he'd been alone for too long. He was used to it, and he liked not having to think of anyone else, but it might have been *too* long. Maybe once he dropped Sabin off at the palace, he'd find someone to spend the night with. If Berith paid him as handsomely as Sabin had said, he'd have the money to do so.

In the meantime, the only thing he could do was continue walking as Sabin talked to him. It wouldn't be as much of a hardship as he'd expected, and Zeno found himself smiling.

CHAPTER SIX

Sabin was exhausted, but he kept putting one hoof in front of the other. No matter how much he wished, there was no other choice. He'd stopped talking, though, and all his energy was going into moving his body. At least the sun was going down. He supposed they would continue walking in the darkness, even though he didn't like it. Zeno was there, and he'd protect him.

He just wasn't sure his body could continue. He felt like eventually it would break, and it wouldn't take long.

His legs felt heavy. They'd gone past the point of hurting, and now, they were numb. He suspected that if he sat down, he wouldn't be able to get up anytime soon, which was why he'd stayed upright the last time they'd stopped to drink. Zeno hadn't asked why, and he hadn't pushed Sabin to sit down. Maybe he knew. He'd been walking right along with Sabin, after all.

But Zeno was used to it. The longest walk Sabin took in his everyday life was from his rooms to his office. Maybe it was time for him to start exercising or something. He clearly needed it.

Something moved ahead of them, and Zeno froze. He quickly grabbed Sabin's arm and pushed him behind his back, and Sabin went without arguing. He wasn't an idiot. Whatever was moving ahead of them, he had pretty much zero chances of winning the fight. On the other hand, Zeno had killed a dozen demons without breaking a sweat—all of that while Sabin cowered in a corner. If someone was going to attack, Zeno was their best chance.

Still, Sabin hoped no one was about to attack. He didn't have the energy to run for his life anymore.

He squeezed Zeno's arm and looked around him. With the darkness quickly falling, he could only see shapes. There was a big boulder right next to the tiny road they'd started following a while back, and Sabin wished they'd found it sooner. It could have provided some shade, which he sorely needed. His legs weren't the only things that hurt. Every inch of his skin felt tight and hot.

"Put down your bags, and we won't kill you," a voice said.

Sabin's heart raced. So, he *had* seen something moving, and that something didn't want anything good. The demon talking, whoever he was, was trying to rob them.

It was a regular occurrence here in the desert. No matter how many times Berith tried to do something about it, nothing worked for long. There was no way for him to make the entire desert secure, and he'd given up.

This was the result. Sabin would make sure Berith knew how displeased he was that he'd been attacked on his way home.

Sabin hesitated, wondering if they were supposed to obey. Zeno wasn't moving, so he didn't, either, and he waited to see what Zeno would do.

Something moved again behind the boulder, and the demon came into view. Since he probably was the demon who'd been talking, Sabin thought he was male. He didn't have horns, but he did have wings, and they opened behind him, almost as if the demon was trying to be intimidating.

It was working.

Sabin shuddered and pushed closer to Zeno. Then more movement caught his attention, and he sucked in a breath when he saw a second demon come around the boulder. This one had horns, as well as a sword.

Sabin and Zeno were in trouble.

Sabin prayed Zeno wouldn't have a problem taking care of the two demons. Surely they were nothing next to the thirteen demons Zeno had killed just a few hours ago. The only thing Sabin could do was run away screaming, and he doubted that would be of any help. But Zeno was strong and lethal, and he could do this. Sabin knew he could.

With a start, Sabin realized that he and Zeno had been walking for one day. He felt like he'd known Zeno forever and like he'd been stuck in the desert for just as long. Instead, it had been only a handful of hours.

"What do you want?" Zeno asked. He didn't move to retrieve his weapons.

"Your bags and anything of value you have on you," the demon with the wings said. "If you're lucky, we won't kill you."

To Sabin's astonishment, Zeno reached up with both his hands. He wasn't taking out his weapons, but instead, he was pulling down his hood.

What on earth was happening?

Sabin wanted to walk around Zeno and look at him in the eyes, but he didn't dare do so. There had to be a good reason Zeno was showing his face to these demons, and if it was that they were about to die, Sabin didn't want to have the same fate. Maybe whoever saw Zeno's face died? Sabin had never heard of anything like that, but there was a first time for everything, especially in Hell.

The second demon scrambled back so quickly that they fell into the sand. A big black cloud of dust surrounded them, but the demon didn't pause. They rushed back behind the boulder, leaving the demon with the wings on his own.

That demon raised his hands. "I apologize," he said in a rush. "I didn't realize it was you."

Sabin blinked. He'd expected the demons to be afraid of Zeno, but this was a bit much. What the fuck did Zeno look like? Was he that scary?

Sabin could only see the back of his head. Considering the horns, he'd imagined an agramon demon. They didn't have hair, so he hadn't expected it. Zeno *did* have hair, though. It was long and black, tied up and lying on the back of his neck. It was the only thing Sabin could see of Zeno's head along with the horns and pointed ears.

Zeno grunted. "Leave us alone."

The demon stumbled backward. "Of course. I apologize again. You usually travel alone, so I didn't expect it to be you."

Sabin was starting to think that this demon knew Zeno. He was visibly terrified of Zeno, and while Sabin didn't understand why, he was glad for it. Maybe it had something to do with the fact that Zeno could kill thirteen demons without breaking a sweat.

Did that mean he should be afraid of Zeno? No matter how many times he thought about the demons Zeno had killed, Sabin was never afraid. He couldn't be, and he didn't think that would change. No matter how many demons Zeno had killed, he'd been nice to Sabin, and he was saving his life.

"Leave," Zeno ordered.

The demon opened his wings and jumped up. He flew until he reached the top of the boulder, then he disappeared behind it, leaving Sabin and Zeno alone. Sabin wanted to walk around Zeno and see his face, but he was afraid it would make Zeno angry. There had to be a good reason Zeno kept his face hidden, and while Sabin didn't think it was because he was ugly, he didn't want to risk Zeno getting angry.

He stayed where he was, but he couldn't keep the words in. "Why did they run that way?"

"They're scared of me," Zeno said. His tone was flat, almost as if he expected Sabin to run away screaming like these two demons had.

Sabin wanted to reassure him, so he patted Zeno's muscular bicep. "Well, *I'm* not afraid of you."

"You might be if you saw my face."

"I doubt I'll ever be afraid of you. I don't care if you have three noses and four eyes. You've been nice to me, and that's all that matters."

Zeno sucked in a breath.

Sabin was stunned when he started turning around, and he stayed as still as he could, afraid to send Zeno running. Zeno was the one turning to face him, but the moment felt fragile. Sabin could die if Zeno abandoned him in the desert, but that wasn't what he was thinking about right now. No, he was thinking that he was about to see Zeno's face, his eyes, and hopefully, his smile.

The hood Zeno had kept over his head the entire time he and Sabin had been together was on his shoulders now. It meant his entire head was exposed, from the tip of his horns to his chin. Sabin had already seen the black hair, but now he could see all of Zeno.

His skin was gray, just like Sabin had suspected. From what he could see in the growing darkness, it was a light gray, not quite the pink of Sabin's skin, but almost. It gave Zeno a washed-out aspect, but not a bad one.

The most striking feature of Zeno's face was his glowing green eyes. Even in the darkness, Sabin couldn't miss them. He'd only ever seen one kind of demon who had glowing green eyes, so he suspected that Zeno had some thelnyss demon in him. There were no signs of wings, so maybe not a lot, but it was definitely there.

Zeno's nose was straight and long, his chin a little pointed, and his face narrower than Sabin had expected. He could see some of the spikes agramon demons sported on Zeno's forehead, but they weren't scary.

Nothing about Zeno was scary.

Zeno stared at Sabin, clearly still expecting Sabin to scream and run away. Instead, Sabin smiled at him. "You're not scary at all." It wasn't a lie. Sabin wasn't afraid.

If anything, he was quite attracted to Zeno and a bit horny.

Zeno had expected Sabin to run away screaming like the other two demons had, and he wasn't sure why it wasn't happening. Why didn't Sabin find him scary? It didn't make any sense, and Zeno was trying to wrap his mind around it and understand.

"I don't scare you?" he asked, still stunned by Sabin's words.

Sabin shook his head. The curtain still covering him slipped to the side, and he tore it off with a huff. The sun was low now, so he wouldn't need its protection until tomorrow morning. It was probably a relief for him to take it off.

"Why would you scare me? I've seen much worse-looking demons and even a few humans."

Zeno snorted. "I never said I was ugly. I thought you'd recognize me." But apparently, Sabin didn't.

The two demons who'd tried to rob them had, but then Zeno thought he'd met them before. He knew a lot of criminals, but as long as he wasn't hired to kill them, he didn't hurt them. It was always good to have allies, even allies he didn't fully trust.

Sabin blinked. In the growing darkness, his eyes looked almost black instead of purple. It was a pity that Zeno couldn't see them well anymore. He kind of liked those eyes, and he especially liked that they weren't full of fear anymore.

"Why would I recognize you? I'm sure I've never seen your face in my life."

"Have you ever heard of The Mercenary?"

Sabin's eyes widened. "Who hasn't? In the past few years, he's become Hell's bogeyman."

Zeno stared. He wouldn't have to spell it out for Sabin to understand. He was pretty sure Sabin was smart enough to realize what Zeno was saying yet not run away. He'd die alone in the desert, and he was very much aware of that.

Zeno hadn't thought it possible, but Sabin's eyes widened even more. "Are you telling me you're The Mercenary?"

Zeno dipped his head in acknowledgment.

Sabin took a step back. He didn't run away, and Zeno didn't blame him for being afraid, but it hurt. He hadn't expected it, and he tried pushing the feeling away. Who cared if Sabin was afraid of him? They weren't friends. Once Sabin was back at the palace, they'd never see each other again. Besides, now that he knew who Zeno was, maybe Sabin would keep his mouth shut as they walked.

Zeno gave a tiny sigh. He hoped Sabin wouldn't shut up. He quite enjoyed listening to him, even though it meant that their presence was being broadcast all over and that Sabin drank water more often than he normally would, which wasn't great since they were in the middle of a desert.

He couldn't decide for Sabin whether or not Sabin should continue following him. He hoped Sabin would, because he'd die otherwise, and Zeno didn't want him to, but trying to talk to Sabin probably wouldn't help. So instead of trying to convince him he wouldn't hurt him, Zeno turned around and started walking again. Sabin would decide if he was too afraid of Zeno to continue walking with him or if he was ready to give it a try.

Zeno walked slowly, listening to the sounds coming from behind him. If Sabin came with him, he'd have questions, and Zeno wasn't sure he could answer them. He'd never talked to anyone about being The Mercenary. He thought the name was a bit stupid, but he hadn't been the one to create it. He was just Zeno, but people had started talking about him and the jobs he got hired to do, and apparently, they'd needed a name. Zeno didn't often give out his, so they'd come up with The Mercenary.

Zeno supposed that was what he was. He sold his services to whoever had enough money to afford them, and while he made sure not to kill innocent demons, he didn't hesitate to do what he'd been hired to do. It had created a reputation, and most of the time, like with the two demons who'd tried to rob them, it was useful. It meant people stayed away from him, but he didn't want *Sabin* to stay away.

What the fuck was happening to him?

He'd been distracted for a few minutes, and now that he tuned back into Sabin, he could hear the sound of Sabin's hooves on the sand. No matter how frightened he was, Sabin was following Zeno, which was what Zeno had wanted.

They were going to have to stop soon, and Zeno had no idea what would happen when they did. He suspected Sabin would ask his questions then, but maybe not if he was too afraid. Zeno wanted to reassure him that he wouldn't hurt him and point out that he'd had plenty of opportunities to do so, but maybe that wouldn't be smart. Was it better to remind Sabin of that or to try to convince him he wasn't dangerous?

Zeno snorted. Who was he trying to fool? He *was* dangerous, and Sabin was very much aware of that. He'd seen him kill a dozen demons without hesitation.

Yet he hadn't run away then, and he wasn't running away now. Sabin was a mystery, and Zeno found himself wanting to unravel it.

Sabin was never silent, so the fact that he couldn't force one word out of his mouth probably meant he was in shock.

And who would blame him?

The Mercenary had a reputation. Even Sabin had heard it, and he barely left the palace. Over the past few years, he'd heard more and more about the demon who people hired to kill other demons or retrieve things that had been stolen from them. The Mercenary was fast, lethal, and silent.

Yep. Zeno was definitely The Mercenary.

Sabin realized that was why Zeno had expected him to be

afraid of him. Maybe he would have been if he'd found out that Zeno was The Mercenary right away, but he hadn't. To him, Zeno was just Zeno, no matter what he was called. It didn't matter that Zeno had killed thousands of demons, even some in front of Sabin. He'd kept Sabin safe, and even though he'd had plenty of opportunities to hurt Sabin and kill him, he hadn't. He'd even caught Sabin several times so Sabin wouldn't fall and hurt himself, for fuck's sake.

No, Zeno wasn't dangerous, at least not to Sabin.

Sabin regretted stepping away when Zeno had told him who he was. More than anything, it had been shock, but he could tell that wasn't what Zeno believed. He thought Sabin was afraid of him, and while there had been a tiny bit of that in the first few minutes, it had vanished.

Sabin wasn't afraid of Zeno—not much, anyway—and he wanted Zeno to be aware of that.

"You know, I wasn't even aware you actually existed," he said.

Zeno's step faltered for a moment, but he continued walking. "What do you mean?"

"That both Berith and I thought it was too much. I mean, there's word of you killing dozens of demons, sometimes at the same time, and we didn't think it was possible."

Sabin snorted loudly.

"Obviously, we were wrong about that. I saw you do it, so I should have realized who you were. I just didn't think you were real."

"I very much am."

Sabin looked Zeno up and down. He could only see the back of the other demon, but he didn't mind. Zeno was nice to look at, especially now that he'd pulled down his hood and Sabin could see his hair. He briefly wondered about the broken horn, but he wasn't about to ask. Considering what he now knew about Zeno, he could imagine how it had been broken.

The horn wasn't what interested Sabin the most, anyway. Zeno was way taller than him, with wide shoulders, a broad chest, and a flat stomach. His ass was round and high, and his thighs were thick.

Sabin licked his lips. What he felt *definitely* wasn't fear.

He cleared his throat. "You're very much real, I agree. Why didn't you kill me when you found me?"

"Why would I kill you?"

"Well, for one, it would have avoided a lot of problems for you. You wouldn't be here, babysitting me in the desert."

"I don't kill innocent demons."

"So you research every single demon you kill?"

"I do. Sometimes, people who shouldn't be there attempt to step in and help, but I try not to kill them."

Sabin might not know much about Zeno, but he could tell Zeno was telling the truth. He wouldn't have expected anything different from him, anyway. Like Zeno had said, he'd had plenty of opportunities to hurt or abandon him, but he hadn't.

"You promise you won't hurt me?" he asked.

"I don't have a reason to. I wasn't paid to hurt you."

Sabin swallowed. "But if you had been, you *would* hurt me." Or kill him, more probably.

Zeno hesitated, but that was all Sabin needed to know the answer.

Okay, so maybe he *was* a bit afraid of Zeno.

But Sabin didn't have a choice. If he wanted to return to the palace, his only chance was Zeno. He could continue following the demon or try to do this on his own, but he could tell how that would end.

He'd die, and soon.

No, his best chance to make it out alive was to be with Zeno, but that meant he had to take a chance. He didn't think Zeno would hurt him, but in the end, he didn't really know the other demon, no matter that he felt like he did. So he could choose certain death in the desert or decide to trust Zeno and go with him.

When he'd followed Zeno, he'd already made his decision, hadn't he? For better or worse, they were stuck together, and Sabin would have to learn to deal with that and with what he now knew of Zeno. He kind of wished he'd never found out Zeno was The Mercenary, though.

Zeno missed Sabin's voice.

He wouldn't have thought it possible when he'd first met Sabin and Sabin had blathered for hours as they walked, but now that Sabin had been quiet for a while, the silence was heavy. Zeno wanted to ask Sabin about the palace, his life there, or about anything he wanted to talk about, but he didn't dare. There was only one reason for Sabin to be silent, and it was that he was afraid of Zeno. Talking to him wouldn't help. If anything, it might make things harder, and that was the last thing they needed.

Zeno shouldn't feel like this, anyway. He always traveled on his own. He was used to silence, and he reveled in it.

Except not this time. What the fuck was wrong with him?

He wasn't surprised that Sabin behaved differently after finding out who he was. Even though Sabin had said he wasn't afraid of him, that had changed once he knew. Zeno had made things even worse by not saying *no* when Sabin asked him if he'd kill him if he were hired to do so. The answer to that question *was* no, and it should have been even when Sabin first asked him.

Sabin wasn't a bad person. He wouldn't hurt a fly, and he didn't deserve to be killed. So if someone had hired Zeno to do that, Zeno would have looked into it and refused the job.

But he wouldn't have told anyone about it. He refused the jobs he didn't want to take, but that didn't mean the people he was asked to kill weren't a target. It was easy for someone to find another demon to carry out a job, and Zeno had learned a long time ago not to feel guilty about it.

But with Sabin, everything was different. Zeno couldn't imagine a world that wasn't brightened by Sabin's presence. His had been, and now it was just a bit dimmer because Sabin was quiet.

Zeno cleared his throat. He saw Sabin jerk back from the corner of his eye, and he told himself not to be hurt by it. He'd startled Sabin, that was all.

"I had plenty of opportunities to kill or hurt you," he said, pointing out the obvious.

"I'm aware of that."

Sabin's voice was soft, but at least he was talking to Zeno. Surely it meant he didn't hate him.

"So you know I won't hurt you," Zeno continued.

"I know you won't hurt me now. But I can't help but wonder what will happen if someone hires you to do so."

So that was what he'd been stuck on. Zeno had suspected it, and now that he knew for sure, he could help Sabin get over his fears. "I wouldn't take the job if someone asked me to kill you."

"Wouldn't you? Because you're The Mercenary. You kill people. It's kind of your thing, and I don't see how I would be any different."

"I already told you I don't kill innocent demons, and I wasn't kidding. If someone hired me to kill you, I'd look into you and refuse the job."

"Why?"

"You seem like a good person. I don't think you've ever killed innocent people or that you would hurt them." Sabin might be the personal assistant to a prince, but that didn't make him dangerous. It did make him vulnerable, but Zeno suspected it was better not to mention that. Sabin was already wary enough of him.

"I like to think I'm a good person. I mean, I made mistakes, like everyone, but the thought of hurting people makes me want to throw up."

"That's what I was saying." Zeno couldn't remember the last time he'd talked so much, but he wasn't done yet. "You don't have to be afraid of me. I realize you don't know or trust me, but you have my word on that. I'll take you back to the palace safe and sound." Even if it was the last thing Zeno did.

"Thank you." Sabin hesitated. "Can I ask some questions about your work?"

Zeno's first instinct was to say no. He didn't want to talk about his job, ever, with anyone. He suspected Sabin was asking because it would make him feel better to know what Zeno did. Zeno wouldn't give him details, but he supposed he could at least reassure him, so he nodded.

Sabin visibly relaxed. Zeno wasn't sure what the fact that he could read Sabin so easily meant, and he wasn't up for exploring those thoughts just yet.

"How did you become The Mercenary?"

Of *course* that was Sabin's first question. "I didn't give myself that name, if that's what you're asking."

"I didn't think you did. You'd never give yourself a name, especially not that one."

Zeno was amused. Sabin thought he knew him well, and maybe in a way, he did. That was astonishing, considering they'd only known each other for a day, if even that. "I wouldn't?"

Sabin shook his head and stumbled. Zeno reached for him, but Sabin was already steady on his hooves again, and Zeno didn't have the excuse to touch him.

"It's ostentatious. I don't think you'd give anyone your real name, but you wouldn't give yourself a nickname or something like The Mercenary. Besides, you don't need one. People can hire you without knowing your name."

"They did, in the beginning. But I get jobs because people talk to each other, and that's what they started calling me. I can't say I like the name, but I don't care if people use it."

"Do you care about being feared?"

Zeno wished he could see Sabin's expression. It was dark, though, and while eventually they'd have to stop, he wanted to walk a little bit longer. He recognized the area of the desert they were traveling through, and he remembered there were some large flat rocks just a bit ahead of them where they could rest. It would take them off the sand, which was always a good thing, especially during the night when the predators came out to play. Most of them lived deep in the sand, slept there during the day, and came out at night to feed.

"Well, having people fear me means they leave me alone," he began.

Sabin snorted. "Why am I not surprised that that's what you care about? Do you really hate people?"

"Most of them. They're annoying, boring, and always insist on asking questions."

"Like me, then."

"A bit. But while you're afraid of me, you're not running away screaming. You're still walking with me, and I appreciate that. You're much stronger than I gave you credit for in the beginning."

Sabin was silent for a moment. "You know, I thought about running away when you first told me who you were."

"But you didn't."

"I had to choose between risking having you kill me or dying in the desert. It wasn't much of a choice."

"I can see that. But you're talking to me. You're asking me questions people haven't dared ask me, ever. You might be afraid of me, but you're not terrified like I expected."

"I probably should be more afraid, but I kind of like you."

Zeno sucked in a breath. He hadn't expected that confession. "You do?"

"You're growly and quiet, but you've only been nice to me. Rationally, I realize it doesn't mean anything and that you might be trying to fool me into trusting you to hurt me, but emotionally, I don't think you will. I just hope my emotions aren't wrong."

"I promise I won't hurt you." Zeno didn't mind repeating himself if that was what Sabin needed.

"And I believe you, no matter how stupid that sounds."

If Zeno had been anyone else, he would have told Sabin he shouldn't trust him or any stranger he met in the desert. But he wanted Sabin to be relaxed with him and to believe and trust him. It didn't make sense, but it was what it was, and Zeno had learned a long time ago to go follow his instincts.

Right now, they were telling him to make Sabin as comfortable as possible. It didn't matter that it didn't make sense. It was what Zeno wanted, and considering how little time they'd have together, that was what he'd do. Besides, things would be easier if Sabin was relaxed rather than fearful. It would take them several days to reach the palace, and things could get awkward if Sabin was freaking out about being killed every time he closed his eyes.

"I won't hurt you," Zeno repeated.

"I know," Sabin murmured.

Then they were silent, but that was fine with Zeno. They'd talked things out, and Sabin didn't fear him as much as he had before. That was a win in Zeno's book, and that was all Zeno had wanted.

CHAPTER SEVEN

Sabin almost fell to his knees to kiss the ground. He could see the palace in the distance, and he had to resist the urge to run ahead in his haste to get there.

He and Zeno had been traveling for days. Sabin had lost count, but now that he was home, he didn't care. It could have been weeks, and he still wouldn't. The important thing was that he was *home* and that he'd be able to take a bath, eat food, and finally sleep in his bed.

He bounced a little. "We're almost there," he told Zeno.

Zeno's hood was up again. Over the past day, they'd been traveling on the road, which meant they'd crossed paths with other travelers. Zeno had decided to stay hidden, which made sense considering what Sabin knew about him. Few people would probably recognize Zeno's face, but just in case, it was better if he hid it. Sabin had done the same with his curtain. At the very least, it meant the sun hadn't burned his skin.

"I can see that," Zeno said. He sounded amused, which was a relief.

Sabin had been learning Zeno's expressions and tone when he spoke, and he was starting to recognize them. When Zeno talked to him, there was an intensity and a lilt in his tone that was there only with him. He didn't know what it meant, but it wasn't helping his stupid crush on The Mercenary.

He still couldn't believe Zeno was The Mercenary. Well, he could believe it after seeing Zeno kill all those demons, but Zeno wasn't anything like Sabin had imagined when he thought about The Mercenary. He was quiet and strong, and he listened to whatever Sabin had to say. Sabin had done most of the talking when he'd relaxed after the big reveal, but even though Zeno hadn't said much, Sabin had known he was listening.

When it came to Zeno, all of his fears had flown out the window. There was no way Sabin could be afraid of him after what they'd gone through together. Zeno had taken care of him. He'd saved him from death, or possibly something even worse. He'd kept him safe, and he'd brought him home like he'd promised.

How could Sabin be afraid of him?

"How long do you think it will take us to reach the palace?" he asked.

"Shouldn't you be the one telling me that? This is your home, not mine."

"But you're the expert traveler." Sabin could see the palace, but it was still too far away for him to be entirely happy. He hoped they'd reach it before night fell, but he realized Zeno couldn't make promises when it came to that.

Zeno hummed. The first time he'd heard the sound, Sabin had been stunned, but he suspected that Zeno didn't even realize he made it when he was thinking. He was comfortable enough with Sabin that he didn't think about what he did or said every second of every day like he had in the beginning, and that knowledge did something to Sabin. He *wanted* Zeno to be comfortable with him. He wanted Zeno to like him, and he thought the other demon did.

The problem was that now that Sabin was home, Zeno would be leaving.

Sabin had been trying hard not to think about it, but he couldn't avoid it anymore. He was almost home, with the palace standing there in the distance.

What would Zeno do once Sabin was home? Would he head out right away, or would Sabin be able to convince him to come inside and rest for a few days? Zeno seemed like the kind of person who didn't rest, but hopefully, Sabin would be able to convince him. He wanted more time with Zeno, even though it wouldn't help.

"Several hours, at least," Zeno said.

Sabin had almost forgotten that he'd asked him a question. "I wish I was already home."

"It won't be long. Come on. The sooner we start walking again, the sooner you'll be home."

Sabin nodded and followed him when he started walking again. His mind was going a mile a minute, trying to find a reason to get Zeno to stay instead of leaving right away. If anything, he'd have to stick around until Berith paid him for saving Sabin and bringing him home. Maybe Sabin could convince Berith to delay that until tomorrow at least, or even a few days. It was the least Berith owed him after he'd gotten him in trouble.

"I can't wait to take a bath," Sabin said. He'd started filling the silence again, but it wasn't because he was uncomfortable anymore. He suspected Zeno enjoyed hearing what he had to say, which was the main reason he was doing it. Zeno would never admit it out loud, and Sabin hoped he wasn't wrong. Knowing Zeno, he'd probably have said something about it if he'd wanted Sabin to stop talking.

"You seem to like your baths," Zeno said.

"What's not to like? You get to sit in nice-smelling water, get clean, and relax at the same time."

"You don't work in the bath?"

"That should be forbidden. Baths aren't made to work. They're made for relaxing."

"I see. So the first thing you'll do is take a bath?"

"Yes. I'll have the servants bring me food and eat while I get clean. I'll stay there for hours. I'll probably have to slather lotion all over me once I'm done. My skin feels tight, and I hate it."

"The desert will do that to you."

And it would have done much worse if it hadn't been for Zeno.

"I want to thank you," Sabin said more quietly. Now that they were close to the city, there were more travelers around, and he didn't want them to overhear what he had to say.

"You don't have to."

"But I do. It would have been easier for you to leave me in the desert. Helping me was something you did out of the goodness of your heart, and I'll always be grateful. I'm not an idiot. I know I'd be dead if it weren't for you, or worse." A few times, Sabin had had nightmares about it. He was sheltered in the palace, but he worked with Berith, so he'd seen his fair share of horrors and had heard about even more of them.

Death was easy. There were plenty of things demons could do to each other that didn't include death but would make them want to die.

"You offered me money," Zeno pointed out.

"I don't think you did this for the money." Sabin could be wrong, but he didn't believe he was. Still, if using the reward to keep Zeno with him for a bit longer worked, he'd do it. "But even if you did, I'm still grateful."

Zeno grunted. They were walking a bit faster now, but Sabin didn't find it as hard as he would have in the beginning. A lot of it had to do with the fact that they were walking on a road now and seeing the city in the distance. Sabin couldn't wait to get there.

With so many more people on the road, he and Zeno now stayed silent as they walked. Sabin had to resist the urge to talk, but he didn't want people around them to recognize him. His head was still covered with the curtain, and he intended to keep things that way until they reached the palace.

He wasn't part of Berith's family, but he couldn't dismiss the fact that someone might try to take him. Berith had to be going nuts right now, with no news of Sabin. Sabin had left his tablet and everything else in the cart because it would have been useless in the desert, and he wouldn't be surprised if Berith had sent people out to find him once he'd realized something was wrong.

If he hadn't, Sabin was going to kick his ass.

Zeno tensed more the closer they got to the city. Sabin took the lead once they reached it and were walking inside the walls. He suspected Zeno was tempted to bow out and tell him to head home on his own, but Sabin would have none of that. When he and Zeno almost got separated by the growing crowd, he grabbed Zeno's hand and pulled him along.

It was big, firm, and warm. The skin scraped against Sabin's more delicate palm, but it made him shudder in pleasure instead of disgusting him. He could only imagine what that would feel like on the rest of his body, and he was tempted to ask Zeno if he wanted to give it a try.

But he couldn't face rejection. Zeno was fond of him, but Sabin didn't have much time with him. As soon as Zeno had everything he needed, he'd leave, and if Sabin allowed him to, he'd take Sabin's heart with him.

Sabin would already be in enough pain as it was. He couldn't get closer to Zeno or fall in love with him.

Although he suspected that he already was.

Zeno had to work hard to resist the urge to turn around and leave the city. Even when he wasn't home on his own, he stuck to small towns. Cities weren't his thing, with so many people around. He despised crowds and would have been happier staying out in the desert.

But Sabin didn't belong there. Sabin belonged *here*, in the palace, in the middle of a bustling city, and Zeno could see him relax more and more as they got closer to the tall walls that surrounded the palace.

No matter how fond he was of Sabin and what he'd

imagined could happen between them, seeing Sabin here reminded him of how different they were. There was no way for them to make it work, no matter how much he might wish for it. Besides, he doubted Sabin wanted the same thing.

Zeno knew himself. He knew how most people saw him, and while Sabin was different, there still was no way he'd ever want someone as grumpy and quiet as Zeno. Zeno had no doubt that they could have sex, but Sabin deserved better. He deserved someone who would stay by his side and love him, and Zeno couldn't do that.

"You'll see, the food is incredible." Sabin was babbling as he pulled Zeno along.

Zeno had been stunned when Sabin had taken his hand, but it made sense. With so many people around, pushing them this way and that, they would have risked losing each other. Zeno didn't care about the reward, but he wanted to make sure Sabin got to the palace safely, which meant he had to stay with him for as long as possible. He was tempted to step away as soon as they reached the walls, but he doubted Sabin would allow him to. Sabin was a force of nature, even though he didn't seem to realize it himself.

"And there are plenty of guestrooms," Sabin was saying. "I know the palace isn't your thing and that you're more comfortable in the desert, but surely, even you can take a few days to rest? We walked a lot over the past few days, and you had to kill thirteen demons. I'm sure you need food and a soft bed."

Zeno didn't think he'd ever had a soft bed. Even when he was home in his shack, he slept on the floor. He had a blanket and a pillow, and that was that. He wouldn't say no to food, though. He despised cooking, and considering he lived in the middle of nowhere in a shack, he didn't have access to much. He hunted sometimes and roasted the meat on a fire, and he couldn't deny he was curious about the kind of food the palace would offer.

That was all he was curious about when it came to the palace. He wasn't afraid of meeting the prince or having to deal with whatever was waiting behind those walls, but he wished he didn't have to.

They reached the wall. Zeno swallowed, knowing they were almost there, but Sabin continued pulling him to the side this time. They walked and walked, the path made harder with so many people walking around them, but eventually, they reached a gate.

"This isn't the main entrance," Sabin told Zeno. "I didn't want people to see us, and they'd no doubt have been curious if we'd gone up to the guards there."

"This is a secondary entrance?"

Sabin nodded. "It's the servants' entrance. I usually use this one to come and go."

Zeno was relieved Sabin had thought about that, because he hadn't. He had no idea how the palace worked, but he supposed it made sense that the servants didn't use the same entrance as the prince.

He wasn't surprised to see two guards standing by the small gate. They were alert, and one noticed them before they even reached the gate. Her back went ramrod straight, and she stared. The prince was well protected, which meant that Sabin was, too. Zeno felt better, knowing that. Soon, he wouldn't be here to protect Sabin anymore, and it helped to know that someone else would.

Sabin stopped in front of the guards. They'd both seen him now, and they waited, staring at him. He reached for the curtain that still covered his face and untied it, but he didn't take it off entirely. He opened it just enough that the guards could see him, and clearly, they recognized him because their eyes went wide.

"The prince has been looking for you," the first guard said.

"I sure hope he has been. Does he think I'm dead?"

The guard reached for the gate and unlocked it. "I think he

hopes you're not. He'll be happy to see you."

"And I'll be happy to see him."

The guards allowed Sabin to walk through the gate, and they didn't have anything to say when he pulled Zeno along. They didn't even ask for Zeno's name, which made Zeno grumble. How could they protect Sabin if they didn't even know who was walking into the palace?

"Stop being grumpy," Sabin said.

"I haven't said anything."

"Maybe not, but I can hear you think. They didn't ask who you are because you're with me. I wouldn't bring home anyone dangerous."

Zeno wanted to point out that he *was* dangerous, but he was stunned silent by the sight in front of him.

He expected the palace to be luxurious, and it was. Considering that this was the servants' entrance, he could barely imagine what the rest of the palace looked like.

The courtyard was small, but it was filled with plants, and there was a fountain in the middle. Zeno had never seen a fountain. There wasn't enough water in the desert to waste it like that.

Several benches were scattered around the courtyard, some in the shade, others in the sun. A few were occupied, and when Sabin took off the curtain, the people sitting on them stared. However, Sabin didn't pause to reassure them that he was all right. He strode toward the palace entrance as if he owned it, and Zeno supposed that in a way, he did. This was Sabin's home, and he was in his element here, while Zeno definitely wasn't. Their roles had been reversed, and Zeno wasn't sure how to feel about that.

Sabin walked into the palace, Zeno still following him. He was tempted to vanish and leave Sabin, but Sabin would never forgive him if he did that. He didn't understand why it was so important to him that he and Sabin left each other on good terms, but he didn't want to ruin their friendship, even if they never saw each other again.

Sabin walked faster as they moved from what had obviously been the servants' quarters to more elegant hallways. Zeno and Sabin seemed out of place here because they were dirty and dragging sand all over, but Sabin didn't seem to care. No one dared stop them until they got to a gate. Zeno had seen the two guards standing there before they reached it. They tensed when they heard Sabin, but just like the guards at the gate, their eyes widened and they gaped when they recognized him.

"He's in?" Sabin asked.

"He is," one of the guards confirmed.

Sabin nodded and reached for the door. The guards didn't react, and Sabin pushed open the door and strode in. Zeno followed him because there was nothing else he could do, but he kept his hood up, just in case.

The room they walked into was an office. It was wide, with big doors that opened onto another garden. A slight breeze made the curtains move, and the air smelled of flowers Zeno couldn't see. The office had a small sitting area by a window, with several armchairs and a table, big shelves heavy with books and scrolls. On the other side, a desk sat with three chairs in front of it. Sitting behind the desk was a demon who shot to his feet when Sabin walked in.

"Sabin?" the demon asked. He scrambled around the desk and threw himself at Sabin.

Zeno kept his distance, but he hovered close in case something happened to Sabin. That was ridiculous, because Sabin was home now, and Zeno was pretty sure that the man hugging him was the prince Sabin worked for, Berith.

He was tall, with pointed ears, long white hair, and dark eyes. Two horns rose above his head, and to Zeno's surprise, his skin was gray, just like his. Berith was slender, but there was an air of danger around him that told Zeno that he wouldn't have a problem defending himself or killing someone.

Zeno just hoped that someone wouldn't be him.

Sabin clung to Berith. He closed his eyes and took a deep breath, and the familiar scent of his friend settled something inside him.

He was home.

Berith buried his fingers into Sabin's hair and pulled him away so he could look at him. "What happened to you? When I didn't hear from you, I sent guards into the desert to find you, but we couldn't. We found the carts, but they were empty, and there was no one around."

Zeno had mentioned something about the bodies of the guards getting eaten, but Sabin hadn't thought about it again until now. He could only imagine what Berith had thought when the guards had found the carts abandoned.

"We were attacked," he explained.

Berith took a step back, but he didn't release Sabin entirely. He kept an arm around his waist, and using his hold, he guided Sabin toward the armchairs by the window. "You look awful."

Sabin snorted. "Thank you so much. I don't know what I'd do without you."

"You know what I mean. You said you were attacked?"

"I was. I thought I'd die in the desert."

"But you're here."

Sabin could only imagine what he looked like. He wasn't looking forward to seeing his reflection once he got to his bathroom, but now wasn't the time to think about how burned his face was. He dropped into one of the armchairs, relieved to finally be able to give his legs a rest.

When he looked up, Berith leaned over him, worry etched in his expression. Behind him stood Zeno, his hood still up, looking like he might run away at any second.

Sabin wouldn't allow him to.

He held out a hand, directing Berith's attention from him to Zeno. "I'm only alive because of Zeno," he explained.

Berith stood tall and faced Zeno. "Whoever you are, thank you. You saved Sabin, and I'll reward you handsomely for that."

Zeno didn't move, shuffle his feet, or do anything that would show he was uncomfortable, but Sabin could tell he was. He wanted Zeno closer, so he wiggled his fingers until Zeno huffed and finally moved.

"Sit down," Sabin ordered. "We've been walking for days."

"I want to know everything that happened to you," Berith said. "But first, I'm calling the healer. I also have to let Lon and Mel know that you're all right. Mel has been beside himself with worry since we realized something had happened to you, and he hasn't slept since then."

Sabin's chest squeezed. Mel cared about him, but knowing he'd been so worried touched Sabin. "I don't need a healer, but I wouldn't mind seeing Mel and Lon."

"I don't care what you think you need or don't need, but the healer *will* see you, and that's that." Berith's voice had a hint of authority to it, something he didn't usually use with Sabin. Sabin might be his personal assistant, but first and foremost, they were friends.

Sabin could tell Berith wouldn't let this go, so he nodded. "Fine. Call the healer. He won't have anything to do because I'm perfectly fine. Zeno protected me."

Berith's gaze held questions Sabin couldn't answer right now. He didn't ask them, and instead, he strode to the doors and threw them open. The guards were there, waiting for his orders.

Sabin leaned toward Zeno. "Are you all right?"

"*I* should ask *you* that. I'm used to the desert. You're not, and you spent several days there."

Sabin waved his words away. "My entire body hurts, but

that's because I'm not used to walking so much. I'll be fine. What about you? I know this isn't your kind of place, but I'm glad you decided to stick around."

"You didn't exactly give me a choice when you took my hand and pulled me along."

Zeno sounded amused, which was a relief. Sabin didn't know what he'd do if Zeno was angry at him or if he decided to leave right away.

The sound of someone running down the hallway made Sabin sit up. He grinned when Mel burst into the office, looked around until he found him, then rushed toward him. Clearly, word had already gotten around that Sabin was home.

Mel scrambled into Sabin's lap and wrapped his arms around him. He buried his face against Sabin's neck, and when Sabin hugged him back, he felt Mel's chest shake with a sob. Sabin's eyes filled with tears, and once again, he took a deep breath.

"I'm all right," he promised.

Mel's arms tightened around him. "I thought you were dead."

"But I'm not. I'm home."

Mel nodded, but he didn't let go of Sabin. Sabin was stunned at how hard Mel was taking this, but maybe he shouldn't be. The human had always been sensitive. He'd even thought about leaving Hell and going back to the human realm because he wasn't sure he could deal with the harshness and cruelty of demons' lives. Sabin was glad Mel had decided to stay. He made Berith happy, and Sabin would have missed him if he'd left.

Sabin could feel Zeno's gaze on him, so he looked up. The hood was still in place, but Sabin could tell Zeno was intrigued by Mel. From what Sabin had gathered, Zeno had never left Hell, but then most demons didn't. He might have seen a few humans, but Hell's humans were all enslaved. as far as Sabin knew. Mel was the only one who wasn't, and he certainly was the only human who was the consort to a prince of Hell.

Sabin patted Mel's back. "I want you to meet someone," he said.

Mel sniffled and leaned back. He seemed to finally realize that he was in Sabin's lap, and his cheeks flushed adorably. He scrambled to get up, and Sabin gently pushed him into one of the empty armchairs.

"This is Zeno," Sabin explained, pointing at the demon who'd saved his life. "When the convoy was attacked, he saved me. The guards did their best, but they weren't enough, and I thought I was going to die. The demons who attacked us thought Berith was in the cart, but instead, they found me. I tried to convince them to keep me for ransom, but I'm not sure they wouldn't have hurt me, even if they had. But Zeno happened to be around, and he stepped in."

"You killed them?" Berith asked.

Apparently, he was done talking to the guards. He'd moved closer again, and his arms were crossed over his chest. He was intimidating, and Sabin suspected that if Zeno had been anyone else, he'd have already left, if anything so he wouldn't have to deal with Berith.

"I did," Zeno confirmed.

"Good."

Sabin wondered if he should tell Berith that Zeno was The Mercenary. He didn't want anyone to freak out or for Berith to decide that Zeno needed to go. Now definitely wasn't the right time to tell him, but Sabin couldn't keep it a secret forever. Berith would kick his ass if he never told him, but he wouldn't understand that Zeno wasn't a danger to anyone in the palace if Sabin admitted the truth.

"Thank you," Mel said.

He reached for Zeno and grabbed his hand. Sabin sucked in a breath, half expecting Zeno to snatch it away, but he didn't. Maybe he realized that Mel was more fragile than a demon, or maybe he was afraid of what Berith would do. Sabin had told him that Berith and Mel were very much in love and that Mel was most of Berith's life. Zeno had to remember that.

"You saved Sabin's life," Mel continued. He twisted to look at Berith. "How are we going to repay him?"

Berith opened his hands. "In any way he wants."

"I don't want anything," Zeno said, and now, he did pull his hand away. "I didn't do much."

Sabin snorted. He might not want Berith to realize who Zeno was right now, but that didn't mean he wouldn't tell Berith what Zeno had done. "He killed thirteen demons to save me. He guided me through the desert and back home. I would have died if I'd been on my own, but instead, I'm here." He looked straight at Zeno. "You saved my life."

Zeno gave a little shrug as if he truly believed he hadn't done anything much. Sabin was desperate to keep him at the palace for at least a day, so he turned his attention to Berith. "I promised him money."

"He can have as much gold as he wants or needs."

"I'll talk to the accountants."

"Not today," Berith ordered. "Today, you'll see a healer, take a bath, and eat as much food as you can stand. Everything else can wait until tomorrow."

Sabin had what he wanted. Zeno would have to stick around for a bit longer, and Sabin hoped it would be enough for him to get over his crush.

When he looked at Zeno, though, he realized it wouldn't be.

Zeno wished he were anywhere but here. He'd take anything—the desert, his shack, even one of the small towns he frequented.

He'd never been in a palace that was as luxurious as this one, and he'd never met a prince of Hell. He'd also never seen a human like the one staring at him right now. Zeno had no idea what to do about it, so he decided that keeping his mouth shut would be for the better.

As much as he wished he wasn't here, he was also glad he'd be able to spend a bit more time with Sabin. The thought of leaving him bothered Zeno in a way it shouldn't, and he wasn't quite sure what to do about it. He'd leave no matter what happened next. He ought to do it as soon as possible rather than delay the inevitable.

But instead of getting to his feet and telling the people in the room that he needed to go, he stayed where he was. He could feel everyone watching him, and it made his skin crawl, but Sabin wanted him to stay, and as stupid as it was, he was ready to do whatever Sabin wished.

Zeno was in trouble.

Several more people walked into the office. From the looks of it, one was a healer, and he knelt next to Sabin, his hands already digging into the bag he was carrying. Zeno kept an eye on him, but he didn't do anything that would hurt Sabin. Sabin tried to wave him off, but the healer wouldn't have any of that, and Zeno was glad.

Sabin had put up a good front as they walked through the desert, but Zeno took a good look at him now that they were at the palace. Sabin's skin was reddened, burned by the sun, the wind, and the sand. His hair was all over the place, and one of his fingers was bleeding. He was covered in dust.

He looked incredibly good.

Zeno felt out of place, and he was. It became even worse when he turned to look at the prince and found him staring. Zeno didn't wiggle in his armchair, but he certainly felt the need to. The person in front of him could decide whether or not he was allowed to leave. The prince only had to give one order, and Zeno's life could be over.

And it wasn't just that the prince was powerful and rich. Obviously, he knew how to defend himself and, if he needed to, how to kill.

"You protected Sabin all the way here," the prince said.

Zeno nodded curtly. "I did."

"He also seems to like you."

"I don't know that he does."

Zeno was surprised the prince hadn't asked him to pull down his hood. He didn't think anyone would recognize him if he did, so he reached for it. He heard Sabin suck in a breath next to him but didn't let that stop him. If the prince recognized him and realized who he was, Zeno would offer to leave right away. If the prince didn't, Zeno would let Sabin decide when and how he should tell his friends about Zeno.

But the prince didn't say anything. He continued staring, and Zeno could almost see the cogs turning in his brain.

"And Sabin said you killed thirteen demons," the prince continued.

"I killed how many demons I had to save him."

"I'm grateful. It seems that Sabin might need a protector. Is it a job you'd be interested in?"

Zeno blinked. He felt better now that the hood was down and he wasn't so warm, but he wasn't sure he'd heard that right. "What do you mean?"

"My consort has personal bodyguards. They follow him everywhere he goes, including in the palace." The prince hesitated. "Unfortunately, we've had problems with demons getting in and attacking me and the people close to me. Mel is safe, and I can defend myself, but I worry about Sabin."

"You don't have to worry about me," Sabin said. He grunted when the healer poked at a spot on his arm. "No one has ever attacked me in the palace. I'll be fine. I don't need anyone to protect me."

Zeno was stunned to realize he was tempted to say yes. It would give him a regular income, a safe place to live, and the possibility of staying with Sabin. Any other demon would have jumped on the opportunity, but Zeno didn't.

The palace wasn't for him. He didn't belong here, and that would become apparent the longer he stayed. Sabin might want him to stay, but he also might not. Right now, he was grateful and relieved to be home, but soon enough, he'd go back to his normal life, and he'd forget all about Zeno.

That would be for the best. Zeno didn't think he'd ever forget Sabin, but he did want Sabin to forget him. Sabin was home, and he could go back to his life. He *should* go back to it. That was why Zeno had taken him all the way here, after all.

He just wasn't sure that Sabin truly didn't need body-guards.

"I can't accept the job," he said slowly. "But I'm sure you'll find someone else to protect Sabin."

Sabin glared at him. "I don't need to be protected. I'm at the palace. I'm safe."

"Until the next demon manages to sneak in," the prince said.

He looked worried, which Zeno understood. How could demons keep sneaking into a prince of Hell's palace? Zeno wasn't happy with the thought that if he left, Sabin would be vulnerable, but what other option did he have?

None. No matter how tempting it was to tell the prince he'd stay, he couldn't. It wasn't just because he didn't belong here. What would the prince do when he found out who Zeno was? No one ever wanted Zeno around, which had always been fine with him.

Suddenly, it wasn't anymore, and he didn't know how to deal with it. He knew what he had to do, though.

He had to go home and leave Sabin behind.

CHAPTER EIGHT

Sabin was going to kill Berith after what Berith had just done. How could he have offered Zeno a job protecting him? Sabin didn't need protecting. He wasn't in the desert anymore, and no one would attack him.

Hopefully.

But Berith had been trying to be nice, and Sabin couldn't berate him for that, especially not after what had happened. Still, he added this to the list of reasons he had to kick Berith's ass. They were going to have a conversation once he felt better.

"Leave Zeno alone," he said.

"I wasn't doing anything," Berith protested.

"You were trying to convince him to move here, and he's not going to. Not everyone wants to live in a palace and work for you."

Berith pouted. "No?"

Sabin rolled his eyes. He'd missed this, and not just the comforts of the palace. He'd thought he'd never see Berith and the others again several times, and it hurt. They wouldn't have known what had happened to him if that had been the case, and he could too easily imagine how it would have destroyed them.

Sabin turned his attention to Zeno. "Don't mind him. I know you want to get back on the road as soon as possible, but maybe you can stay the night? You can bathe, eat food, and rest in a bed."

Sabin expected Zeno to say no. They'd become close as they

walked through the desert, but everything had changed now. It wasn't just the two of them anymore, and Sabin suspected that Zeno couldn't wait to run away. The fact that he was still there was a small miracle, although it probably had more to do with the reward Zeno expected than with Sabin.

"All I'm saying is that you should think about it," Berith added. "The offer to move to the palace is on the table. Let me know tomorrow if you're still unavailable for it."

Sabin could have told Berith that Zeno would say no again, but he didn't want to repeat himself. Berith had to learn that not everyone wanted to make him happy, though, and that some did it because they were scared of him. But Sabin wasn't afraid of Berith, and it looked like neither was Zeno, although that made sense. Considering Zeno's reputation, even a prince of Hell didn't scare him.

Sabin leaned forward, ignoring the healer still poking at his skin. It burned, but hopefully, the healer would have lotion or something for Sabin's overly sensitive skin.

"You'll get your money tomorrow morning," he told Zeno. He didn't want Zeno to think he was keeping him here on purpose, although he was.

"I'm not worried about the reward," Zeno said.

"Maybe not, but I know you're looking forward to going home." Even though Zeno never talked about his home.

Sabin hoped it was comfortable and nice, but somehow, he doubted it. From what he'd gathered, Zeno lived alone in the middle of nowhere. He wasn't used to comfort, and while it was hard for Sabin to wrap his mind around the fact that someone would live like that, he understood not everyone was like him.

The tiniest smile appeared on Zeno's lips. "I am, but staying one night won't kill me."

Sabin couldn't do anything but stare, and he did so until the healer poked another sore spot. Then he jerked away, growling at him. The man clearly didn't care one bit what

Sabin thought of him. He stared and stayed still until Sabin settled back into the armchair.

Then he continued poking at him.

Sabin huffed. "I'm fine. You won't find any wounds on me, so could you stop?"

"You're burned."

"I'm aware of that, but don't you have a salve or something that I can slather all over my body? I don't think that continuing to poke at my burned skin is going to help it heal."

The healer seemed put out, but he leaned back, and Sabin breathed easier. The torture was over.

The healer dug into his bag. "I don't know why I bother. You all do whatever you want anyway," he grumbled. "I wonder why you even bother calling me."

Sabin was amused. It was true that lately, they'd needed the healer more often than usual. He didn't blame the demon because he was grumpy, but he *did* blame him for prolonging his pain. Had he really needed to poke at him the way he had?

The healer took a small jar out of his bag and handed it to Sabin. "Here. Slather this all over your body. Ask for help if you need it. I'd offer my expertise, but somehow, I doubt you'd accept. It'll help with the oversensitive feeling and the healing."

"He's all right?" Berith asked.

"Considering what he went through, very much so. I'm surprised that the only medical problem is sunburned skin."

"That was to be expected. He did spend days walking in the desert."

The healer nodded. "Between the sun, the sand, and the wind, it was to be expected."

"You realize I'm sitting next to you and that you could talk to me directly, right?" Sabin asked the healer.

The demon's eyes narrowed. "Oh? *Now* you want to know what I think about this?"

"I never said I didn't want to know what you thought

about my skin," Sabin protested. Who was this demon?

Several healers worked at the palace, and usually, the first one available came when they were needed. Sabin remembered that this one had been coming around lately, which was probably why he was so annoyed.

"Once the jar is empty, come to me, and I'll check your skin again," the healer continued as he got to his feet.

Sabin grabbed his wrist. "Wait."

The healer's expression instantly turned to worry. "What is it? Are you in pain?"

Sabin was glad that was the first thing the healer asked. No matter how grumpy he was, he had his patient's best interest at heart. Sabin suspected he couldn't have said the same about some of the other healers.

"No," Sabin told him. "I'm fine. I just didn't catch your name."

The healer stared for a moment before nodding. "I understand. My name is Reyni."

"I'm sorry you've had so much work to do lately. I'm grateful you helped me and that you didn't kick my ass to keep me still and make me stop complaining."

The tiniest smile played at the corner of Reyni's lips. "It was tempting, but it wouldn't have helped you. Now, if you don't have anything else you need me to care for, I should go."

Sabin let him go, and after nodding both at him and Berith, Reyni turned and headed for the door. Sabin waited until the door was closed behind him to turn to Berith.

"You should give him a raise."

"Maybe even a promotion. I like him."

So did Sabin. He reminded him a bit of Zeno. He was grumpy and didn't talk much, but he cared, and it was obvious in the way he behaved.

"Now, I'm sure you want to go to your rooms," Berith said.

Sabin got to his feet and stretched, wincing when it pulled

on his skin. "I can't wait to get into the bath."

"I'll have someone carry you there."

Sabin glared at Berith. "You will *not*. I've been walking for days. I can walk just a little more if it means reaching my room and finally being able to wash."

"I can call the healer back if you want."

"You can, but he's not going to tell you anything new. I'm fine. My skin is overly sensitive, but it'll pass."

Berith stared for a moment, then to Sabin's surprise, he pulled him into another hug. This one was more careful, as if Berith was afraid Sabin would break. Sabin kind of felt like he might. He'd told himself to stay strong while he was on the road, and he had. Now that he was home, he felt like he might break.

He just didn't want to do it in Berith's arms.

It wasn't that he was ashamed or that he didn't want Berith to see him cry. But Berith had worried so much about him already, and Sabin didn't want him to continue doing so. He'd be fine. He was overwhelmed by everything that happened, but a good cry would be enough for him to feel better. If he cried in front of Berith, Berith would freak out and try to fix him, and that was the last thing Sabin needed.

He patted Berith's back, then gently pushed him away. "I stink."

Berith laughed. "You really do."

"Which is why I need a bath. I promise I'm fine. Stop worrying about me, all right?"

Berith's expression was serious. "I don't think I can ever do that, but I'll try. It's good to have you home, Sabin."

"It's good to be home." Even though it meant that soon Zeno would be leaving. Sabin would deal with that once he was on his own in his room, though.

Zeno felt incredibly out of place, and he was. He couldn't

believe Berith had offered him a job, but he already knew he'd say no to the offer. He couldn't stay, no matter how much he wanted to.

And he was surprised to find out that he did want to. For the first time, it was tempting to let go of his job as a mercenary, move into the palace, and not have to worry about being attacked or having to take a job he disliked because if he didn't, he wouldn't eat. He could stick around Sabin, get to know him, and maybe, something could blossom between them.

But no. No matter how much he wanted to, Zeno could never stay. He'd be out of place here, and eventually, it would ruin everything. He wasn't someone who could live with other demons. He'd never been, and attempting to do so would only ruin what he and Sabin had.

But for one night, he could stick around. He'd never been in a place like this, and he couldn't deny he was looking forward to eating delicious food and even the bath thing. Sabin had talked about his baths every day since they'd met, and Zeno was curious. This was his only chance to see the place where Sabin lived and to spend just a bit more time with him.

Zeno wouldn't waste it.

Sabin turned toward him. "Come on. I'll show you to a guest room. You can take a bath and have food brought to you. I doubt you'll be up to eating with Berith and the rest of the group."

There was nothing Zeno wanted less than to eat with a bunch of people he didn't know. Things might have been different if dinner had been only with Sabin, but from the way he talked, Zeno doubted he'd be going anywhere but his room tonight.

It was good. Sabin needed rest, not to have to explain to a bunch of people what had happened to him. They could bother him tomorrow. Tonight, Sabin had to focus on himself and feeling better.

"I can have a servant show him to his room," Berith intervened.

Sabin glared at him. He didn't seem to be afraid of the prince, which had surprised Zeno. As he watched them together, though, he realized that there was a deep friendship between them, much more than should be between a prince and his personal assistant. Sabin had mentioned that he and Berith were friends, but Zeno hadn't known what to think of it and had thought that maybe, Sabin was exaggerating. Now he knew that wasn't so. They truly were friends, and the prince had been worried.

"I'll show him," Sabin said. "And I know you'll feel the need to hover now I'm home, but don't. I'm perfectly fine, and you don't have to run around after me and check up on me. Stop worrying and focus on what you should be doing."

Berith grinned. "And what's that?"

"Your job. I'm home, so you can focus now."

"How do you know I wasn't focused before?"

Sabin patted the prince's cheek. "Because I know you. You were freaking out about me."

"Of course I was." The prince caught Sabin's hand. "How could I have not? You were missing, and I thought I'd lost you."

"Well, you didn't. I'm back, and I'm not going anywhere, so stop it."

The prince raised both his hands. "All right. If you don't want me to take care of you, I won't."

Sabin rolled his eyes. "That's not what I said, but fine. Don't take care of me. I can take care of myself."

The prince's expression softened. "I know. It doesn't mean you should have to. I'm just happy to have you back and in one piece."

"I'm happy to be back." Sabin sniffed. "I also need a bath, so I'll go. Zeno, I'll show you to one of the guestrooms on my way. I'm sure you're dying for a bath, too."

Zeno had never taken a bath, not unless he counted the times he'd swum in a lake. He could guess baths were very different, and while he could already tell they wouldn't be his thing, for one night, he could indulge.

He turned to the prince. "Thank you," he said.

Berith waved Zeno's words away. "I'm still the one thanking you. Without you, we would have lost Sabin, and I don't know what I would have done then. You'll get your reward tomorrow, and I want you to think about what you want. You can ask for pretty much anything, and if it's in my power, I'll give it to you."

That was how important Sabin was to the prince. Nothing surprised Zeno anymore, or at least he'd thought so. But Sabin was unique and special. Every time he opened his mouth, Zeno was surprised. He never expected anything Sabin said.

Sabin took Zeno's hand and dragged him toward the doors that opened in the garden rather than the one from which they'd entered the office. "We're going," he told the people in the room. "I know you all want to talk to me and make sure I'm all right, and I swear I am. I missed you, and I'll be glad to talk to you tomorrow. Right now, I'm going to wash, eat, and sleep for twelve hours. Berith, I hope you don't expect me to be at work tomorrow morning, because I doubt I'll be up for it."

"Take as much time as you need," Berith said, sounding amused. He clearly was used to Sabin's antics.

"Oh, I will. I didn't need your permission, and I wasn't asking for it. I was warning you."

The sound of Berith's laughter followed Sabin and Zeno out of the office and into the garden.

Zeno looked around as soon as they stepped out of the palace. The garden was like nothing he'd seen before, and it was amazing. Everywhere he looked, there were plants, fountains, and benches. He was used to the desert, and he didn't know where to look.

"It's beautiful, isn't it?" Sabin asked softly.

"It is."

"You know, I always took all of this for granted. I've been living at the palace for years, and while my family is nowhere near as rich as Berith, we're okay. We have a home, and it's nicely decorated and everything. But being out there in the desert has shown me how lucky I am."

"Because you could have died."

Sabin snorted. "Because I could have died, yes, but also because of all of this. Most demons will never see so many plants. Most demons don't even know what a fountain is. I never realized how privileged I am, but now, I do."

Zeno didn't say anything. He didn't need to. He agreed that Sabin was privileged, and it was good that Sabin had realized that. There wasn't much Sabin could do about it, though. Hell was mostly a desert, and it would be impossible to change that.

Sabin shook himself. "Well, I doubt you want me to give you a tour of the palace and gardens, so let's go. I can't wait to flop on my bed and not get up for twelve hours."

"You need a good night's sleep."

"And I'll get it. So will you, so we should go."

Zeno followed Sabin through the garden. It was much bigger than he'd expected, and at one point, he wondered how easy it would be to get lost. The trees got so deep that he couldn't see beyond them, and as he and Sabin walked, it was almost as if they were on their own again.

"I told Berith it was ridiculous to want to include so many trees in the private garden, but he didn't listen to me," Sabin said.

"How big is it?"

"Much too big. The gardeners don't attend to this area of the gardens. It's mostly trees, although there's a little stream if you go that way. It's natural and beautiful, and sometimes, I spend time there."

"You should. It's beautiful."

"It is, and here, I feel like I'm alone. No one ever comes around. I guess most people at the palace don't care about the trees in the garden, or maybe they don't want to walk so far."

"But you do."

Sabin smiled softly. "I love this place. We're still protected at the palace, but we're also isolated. It feels as if we're alone in the world, and I like that."

Zeno did, too, and once again, he wished he could stay.

But this wasn't his life. It was Sabin's, and while Sabin needed to go back to it, Zeno had to go back to his own. It was how things had to go and how they *would* go, no matter how little he liked it.

CHAPTER NINE

Sabin shuffled his feet. He wasn't ready for Zeno to leave, but the time had come.

They should have spent more time together yesterday. Sabin had intended to do so, but he'd fallen asleep as soon as he'd sat on his bed after his bath. He'd woken up when a servant had brought him breakfast this morning, and when she'd told him that Zeno was ready to leave, he'd rushed out without eating. Now, here they were, standing by the servants' entrance at the back of the palace.

Zeno was wearing the same clothes he'd worn during their time together. They'd been washed, and he looked slightly uncomfortable, as if he wasn't used to wearing clean clothes. That was probably the case.

Sabin wanted to offer to wash his clothes every day if it made him stay, but he didn't. He doubted anything he could say would convince Zeno to stay.

Berith gently knocked their shoulders together. "You look like this is a funeral."

"I'm sad that he's leaving."

Zeno was a few feet away, accepting food from a servant. He looked awkward, but Sabin wanted him to be okay as he headed home. The best way to make sure of that was to give him food, as much water as he could carry, and anything else he could need. It wouldn't leave much space for whatever reward he was about to ask from Berith, but Sabin supposed he could have it sent to him.

"Has something happened between the two of you?"

Berith asked. He sounded hesitant, which wasn't like him.

"What do you mean?" Sabin knew what he meant, but he didn't know how to answer.

"I don't have to spell it out for you. Did you sleep with him?"

Sabin shook his head. "No. We didn't do anything like that."

"But you wanted to."

"So? I don't police who you can have sex with."

Berith raised his hands. "I didn't mean anything by it. I'm just trying to understand why you're so distraught at the thought of Zeno leaving."

"What do you care? Does it matter? Zeno saved my life. He kept me safe during the days we had to walk through the desert, and we got to know each other. He's become a friend, which is why I'm sad."

"You're allowed to be sad. I just don't like seeing you this way, especially when I just got you back."

Sabin forced a smile on his lips. "I'll be fine. I just need a little more rest, and I'll be as good as new. You don't have to worry about me."

"I don't think it's possible for me not to worry," Berith murmured.

Zeno turned toward them with his arms full of food. He started stashing it into his bag, but it was too much, and not everything would fit. He had to give some of it back to the servant, but he stepped toward Sabin once his bag was closed.

"I'm ready," he said.

Sabin wasn't, but he nodded anyway. He was relieved when Berith moved forward and gestured at another servant. She came closer and handed him a small bag, and Sabin knew it was filled with gold. Berith held it out to Zeno, who stared at it as if he didn't know what to do with it.

"I know you said you didn't want a reward for bringing Sabin home, but I want you to have something anyway. I hope this will help you in your travel back home, and if you need anything, feel free to contact me. I'll always owe you, no matter how much time passes."

Zeno was still staring at the bag, so Sabin snatched it from Berith's hands and pushed it into Zeno's. Zeno caught it, but he also caught Sabin's fingers.

"It's the least I can give you for what you did for me," Sabin murmured.

"I already told you I didn't do it because I wanted gold."

"You might not want it, but you deserve it. Please. I wish I could give you so much more, but I know you won't accept it. This is the very least I can do."

Zeno looked at Sabin.

Their hands were still touching, and Sabin wanted to scream that it wasn't fair. He hadn't been so attracted and interested in a demon in a long time, and here he was, losing every chance he might have had with Zeno.

"Thank you," Zeno murmured eventually. Sabin let his hand go, and he watched as Zeno hid the bag under his tunic.

"Are you sure you can't accept the job as Sabin's bodyguard?" Berith asked. "I can pay you however much you think you deserve."

"The palace isn't my home," Zeno said. "It was nice to be here for a night, but I don't belong here."

Sabin wanted to scream that he didn't, either, so he'd be allowed to go with Zeno, but it would be a lie. He *did* belong here at the palace. It had been his home for years, and he didn't want to lose it.

The problem was that he also didn't want to lose Zeno.

"I'll go talk to the servants," Berith said. He sounded awkward, and it made Sabin smile because he wasn't used to that coming from his friend. Berith was trying to give him and Zeno space and time to talk, and Sabin was glad, but it wouldn't change anything.

"Thank you again," he whispered once he and Zeno were

relatively alone.

"You have to stop saying that. I did what was right, as anyone would have."

"That's bullshit," Sabin blurted out.

The corner of Zeno's lips curled into a half-smile. "It is," he agreed. "But I did what I had to do, and you don't have to keep thanking me for it. The only important thing is that you're home and safe." Zeno hesitated. "Be happy, Sabin. Live your life, and please, never travel through the desert again."

"You should tell Berith that, but I'll do my best. But you, you have to try to stay alive."

"I'll do my best about that, too. It was great to travel with you."

"I couldn't have asked for a better savior. I enjoyed meeting you."

Sabin wanted to throw himself into Zeno's arms, but he knew better. Zeno wasn't the kind of demon who hugged, so instead, Sabin reached out and quickly squeezed his hand. They stared at each other for a moment longer, and Zeno was the one who took the first step away. Sabin stayed where he was and watched Zeno turn toward the gate. The two guards outside it opened it, and Zeno slipped through. He didn't look back, and Sabin wasn't sure if he was happy about it or sad. Seeing Zeno's face one last time wouldn't have changed what was happening. If anything, it probably would have made it even harder for him to let go.

The guards closed the gates, and the sound made Sabin jerk. It was final.

"Will you be all right?" Berith asked.

Sabin forced himself to turn away. There was nothing left for him to watch. "Of course. Why wouldn't I be?" He tried to sound as if everything was perfect in his life.

Berith didn't look convinced, but then, neither was Sabin. He'd miss Zeno, which was nuts considering how little time they'd spent together. But it was time for Sabin to go back to his everyday life. He was home, as far away from the desert as he possibly could get in Hell, and he needed to focus on what was next, not on what he'd lost.

The sound of the gate closing behind Zeno was final. He resisted the urge to look back to see if he could see Sabin but instead kept his gaze forward. Sabin was somewhere behind him, safe in the palace, and that was all that mattered. Zeno could go back to his life now, and he should have been happy.

He was.

Well, kind of. He was happy to leave the palace because he'd felt incredibly awkward there, surrounded by so many beautiful things, with people serving him and asking him if he needed anything. He'd tolerated it for one night, and he'd even enjoyed the bath and the food, but it was time for him to go back to the desert.

He could almost feel the palace's presence behind him, calling him back. He'd thought about accepting the prince's offer for most of the night, but in the end, he'd done the right thing by saying no. He wasn't a bodyguard. He was better at killing demons than at protecting them, and what would the prince have thought if he'd ever found out who Zeno was? He had to have heard of The Mercenary, and there was no way he would trust Zeno if he found out that was who was at his table. It was better to end things this way, and Zeno kept thinking that as he headed toward the edge of the city.

He didn't have to stop anywhere since he'd had plenty of rest and his bag was full of food and water, so he headed straight for the exit. He felt a bit better once he was in the desert, and when he took a deep breath, it burned his lungs.

He was home.

He started walking. It became easier with every step, and after several hours, he finally allowed himself to turn around.

He could still see the city in the distance, and it called to him, but it was easier to ignore it now. He doubted he'd ever go back, so he stared for a moment, wanting to remember this moment for as long as he could.

He didn't think he'd ever forget Sabin. How could he? Sabin had barged in his life, beautiful and intense, and for a few days, he'd made Zeno *feel*. Zeno hadn't thought it possible, but he couldn't deny it, especially considering how much he missed Sabin. It was probably better that they wouldn't see each other again. Sabin could too easily become a weakness for Zeno, and if Zeno's enemies found out, they'd use it against him. In order to keep Sabin safe, Zeno had to be as far away from him as possible.

So he turned around and started walking again.

He was used to walking in the desert, so it was nothing to him to walk for most of the day. He stopped when he found a little shade and ate lunch under it, and as he did so, he tried to remember how things had been when he was alone. It was odd, but the silence was almost too much for him to bear, even though he'd relished it before. Sabin had filled every moment of every day with his voice, but Zeno shouldn't be used to it already.

Once he was done with lunch, he got back on the road. He was tempted to continue walking through the night, but it could be dangerous, so instead he found a hidden spot behind a bunch of rocks and sat down there. He didn't light a fire because he didn't want to draw attention. Besides, he still had enough food from the palace to feed himself without having to hunt.

If he'd lit a fire or had made any kind of noise, the demons would have noticed him. As it was, he was the one who noticed them, and he held his breath as they walked past the rocks he was behind.

"How are we supposed to get inside the palace?" one of them was asking.

"Why are you talking about this here? Someone could hear us," another one hissed.

"Who? There's no one around."

"He's not wrong," a third voice said. "And I'd like to know how we're supposed to sneak into the palace. I've heard that Berith's home is one of the most protected of all the princes of Hell."

Demon Two snorted. "That's because of that human he's fucking. He doesn't want anyone to hurt him."

"Which means it won't be easy for us to sneak in," Demon Three said.

"It can be easy if you know someone on the inside."

"Who do you know?" Demon One asked.

"None of your business. It'll be easy, though. We go in, find the prince, and kill him. Then we take his place."

"And who's going to be the prince?" Demon One asked.

He didn't sound too bright. Zeno had no idea who these demons were, but even he could tell that Demon Two intended to take the prince's place.

They were planning on killing Berith. Normally, Zeno wouldn't have cared, and he wouldn't have worried. But he'd been at the palace, and Berith had admitted to him that they'd had several break-ins over the past few months. They didn't know who kept letting them in, but clearly, these demons knew who to ask for help. If they managed to get into the palace and reach Berith, there was a chance they'd kill the prince. If that happened, Zeno had no doubt that these demons would kill everyone who belonged to Berith's inner circle and family.

That included Sabin.

Zeno's mouth tasted bitter at the thought. He'd left the palace thinking that Sabin would be safe, but apparently, that wasn't true. He kept thinking about every possible scenario, but they all ended with Sabin being hurt by the demons planning to kill Berith.

Zeno shook his head. It was none of his business. He'd brought Sabin home, and now it was Berith's responsibility to keep Sabin and everyone else safe. No matter how much Zeno liked Sabin, he couldn't protect him for the rest of his life and from all the demons who wanted to kill Berith.

The problem was that thinking about how many people might try to kill the prince made him freak out even more rather than resign him.

"What about everyone else?" Demon one asked. "Isn't the prince's consort supposed to take his place if he dies?"

"His consort is human," Demon Three pointed out. "No one would accept him taking the prince's place. Besides, we're going to kill all of them, so there won't be anyone left to take Berith's throne."

"There won't be anyone but us," Demon Two said.

"I'm tired," Demon One complained.

"You're worse than a child. We're almost in town, so stop bitching and continue walking."

Demon One must have done so, because Zeno listened to their footsteps fade in the desert's darkness. Once he was alone, he got to his feet. His best bet to keep these demons away from Sabin would be to kill them, and he could have done so easily, but then what? There was no way to know if they were the only ones in on this plan, and even if they were, there would be others. Zeno wouldn't be able to do anything about those, but he could help Sabin this time around. If he got to Sabin in time to tell him what was happening, the prince might be able to capture these demons and find out what they were planning. Then he could act accordingly, and Zeno would be able to go home because he'd know Sabin was safe.

He quickly packed his things. He didn't like traveling during the night, but he'd have to risk predators finding him. As long as he got to the palace in time, he'd be fine.

And if he didn't get there in time, the three demons who

had so stupidly talked about their plan to kill a prince of Hell where anyone could hear them would die.

Zeno suspected they'd die either way, but he'd volunteer to do it if anything happened to Sabin.

CHAPTER TEN

"You have a meeting with the accountants tomorrow morning," Sabin said, keeping his focus on his tablet.

The thing had always been an extension of his hand, but he was surprised to realize he hadn't missed it while he'd been in the desert with Zeno. Now, it felt odd to hold it, but it was his job.

Berith had tried to convince him to get more rest, but he hadn't been able to. He needed something to distract himself from the knowledge that he'd lost Zeno, and the best way to do that was to work. So, as of this morning, he and Berith were working again. It was taking Sabin a bit more effort than he'd expected to get back into the mindset, but he'd done this for years. Meeting a handsome demon who'd saved his life and had made him half fall in love with him wouldn't change that.

"I don't like the accountants," Berith complained.

"You don't like anyone who isn't a friend or part of your family," Sabin pointed out. "But you have to meet with them and listen to them this time. I won't take notes." He definitely would. He always took notes, just in case Berith missed something.

"You always take notes. It's your job."

Sabin glared. "And *your* job is to listen to the people talking to you when they are. I mean, I don't think your accountants are eager to meet with you any more than you are to meet with them. It would be better for them if they could work without having to see you, but unfortunately, you're the prince, so you'll listen to what they have to say, nod in the right places, and give them whatever they need."

Berith leaned back in his chair. They were in his office, and all the windows were open. Sabin had to resist the urge to dump everything and run into the garden, go to his stream, and hide there for the rest of the day. At least there was a little wind, and it brought in the smell of the flowers.

"You're grumpy," Berith said. "Does it have to do with a certain demon leaving?"

"I'm grumpy because you won't act as you should."

"You know I'll go to the meeting with the accountants and that I'll listen to them. Whenever am I not a responsible prince?"

Sabin rubbed his face. Berith was right. No matter how much he teased and complained about his responsibilities, he always shouldered them. There was nothing more important to Berith than his family, and to keep them safe, he had to stay on the throne. That meant he had to do all the work a prince needed to do, and he'd never hesitated. Sabin was taking all of this too seriously, and it had to do with Zeno and how he'd taken Zeno leaving.

"Why am I like this?" he asked, not expecting an answer. "I only met him days ago. He saved my life, but still. I shouldn't want to see him again so much."

"I don't think it has anything to do with the fact that he saved you," Berith said. He sounded cautious, as if he expected Sabin to snap at him.

He probably wasn't wrong. Sabin had been in a mood since yesterday, when Zeno had left, and he couldn't see it changing anytime soon.

"Why else would I miss him so much?"

"You're usually very careful with your emotions," Berith said. There was something in his gaze, almost like tenderness. Sabin wasn't used to seeing it aimed at him. Usually, it was reserved for Mel or Cyarea, Berith's daughter.

"That hasn't changed."

"You didn't let me finish. It might not have changed, but *you* have. Zeno means something to you, much more than you've admitted even to yourself. Have you fallen in love with him?"

Sabin's first instinct was to shake his head, and he did. Berith continued staring at him until Sabin had to tell him the truth. "I don't know if I fell in love with him, but it would be easy for me to."

"The time you spent together in the desert pushed you close to him. He was the only person there with you, so maybe it isn't actually love. I'm sure you'll get over it."

But Sabin wasn't so sure. He wanted to get over it because Zeno wasn't coming back, but could he?

A noise from the garden distracted him. He was grateful for it, and he started getting to his feet to move toward the window. He wouldn't close it, but he might peek outside and yell at whoever was disturbing him. It wouldn't be like him, but people would understand. He'd spent days walking in the desert after being attacked and almost killed, after all.

A figure appeared at the open door. Sabin frowned, wondering who dared interrupt the prince in his office without knocking.

He didn't have to wait long to find out. A demon walked in, and Sabin was sure he'd never seen him before. He was wearing dusty, dirty clothes, which meant he wasn't anyone who lived at the palace.

And he wasn't alone. Two demons came in after him, and both Sabin and Berith shot to their feet. "Who are you?" Sabin demanded to know. "What are you doing here? If you want an audience with the prince, you're going to have to contact me and set up an appointment. You can't just walk in like that."

The first demon grinned. "Oh, I'm so sorry I don't have an appointment. I'm sure the prince won't mind, though."

"I do mind," Berith said.

But the demon was already reaching for a knife hanging by his side. Sabin swallowed and realized what was happening.

"How the fuck do you keep getting in?" Berith asked as he threw himself away from his desk and toward the demons.

Sabin scrambled back. He wasn't a fighter. He had no idea what to do, but he knew that nothing he could do would help. It was better for him to stay out of the way, but he couldn't abandon his friend. So he rushed toward the door.

The guards out there were bound to hear the noise eventually, but the sooner Sabin let them know the prince was being attacked, the better it would be.

He never reached the door.

One of the demons caught him by the arm and pulled him back. Sabin cried out and turned to face the demon, swinging his free arm as he did so. The demon was ready for him, and he caught Sabin's wrist, squeezing it to the point of pain.

"Where do you think you're going?" The demon asked.

"Let me go," Sabin snapped.

The demon's smile widened. "Oh, I will. Just not now."

Sabin looked around, desperately needing someone to help him, but Berith was busy. He'd taken on the other two demons, which meant Sabin would have to take care of this one.

He had no idea how to do that.

Apparently, he'd managed to escape the desert and come home only to be killed here, in Berith's office. There was irony in that, but Sabin didn't care to think about it at the moment. He just cared that he was about to lose his life and that everything Zeno had done for him had been in vain.

Zeno grabbed the demon hovering over Sabin and pulled him away, throwing him against the wall. The landing caused a piece of art on the wall to fall on his head, but he was already scrambling to his feet and looking around for Zeno.

Zeno was ready for him.

The demon launched himself at him, and Zeno caught him, grabbing his shoulders, and twisting as he did so. He pushed the demon away, and the demon stumbled, then quickly turned around to face Zeno again.

Zeno was going to kill him.

How dare this demon attack Sabin? Sabin was one of the nicest people Zeno had ever met, and he didn't deserve to be attacked in a place where he was supposed to be safe. He didn't deserve to be attacked at all.

As the demon came back toward him, Zeno took out his knives. When the demon launched himself at him, he slashed his blades, grinning savagely at the sound the demon made. Whoever this demon was, he'd had no idea what he was going against when he decided to attack Sabin. He couldn't have known that Sabin had a protector and that Zeno was more than happy to kill for him.

The demon's body fell to the floor, his head almost severed from his neck. Blood spread under his body, but Zeno had already turned his attention to Sabin. "Are you hurt?"

Sabin shook his head. His eyes were wide, and he pressed a hand against his mouth as if he were trying to keep a scream inside, but thankfully, he didn't seem to be afraid of Zeno. Zeno quickly squeezed Sabin's arm, then turned toward the prince, who'd been fighting two demons when Zeno had barged in.

He wasn't anymore.

Zeno blinked and looked at the two bodies on the floor. The prince stood above them, looking as if he'd barely broken a sweat fighting them. One of the demons was missing an arm, and the prince was still holding it.

"That's disgusting," Sabin said with a huff.

The door flew open, and guards streamed in. Zeno snorted, because it was clearly too late for them to do anything, but it wasn't his place to say it.

The prince pointed the torn-off arm at the guards. "You're

late. Again."

"Our apology, your Majesty," one of the guards said. Her focus jumped from the prince to the bodies on the floor, to Zeno. She stepped toward him, but Sabin placed himself between the two of them. He put his hands on his hips and glared, and the guard frowned at him as if she didn't understand what the problem was.

"The prince and I have been attacked. We were fighting for our lives, and the only reason I'm not dead is that Zeno saved me. I can't say the same about you. You were supposed to be outside the office, ready to act if anything happened. Yet you didn't. Once again, you arrive only after the attackers have been taken care of. Can you explain why?"

The demon's skin was a deep red, so she couldn't blush, but Zeno suspected she would have if she'd been able to. She looked pissed, so Zeno took a step forward, but he didn't need to. She didn't attack Sabin. Instead, she bowed her head. "I apologize. We weren't sure what was happening, and no one called for us."

"Then knock on the door," Sabin said as he threw his hands in the air, clearly frustrated. "Or would you rather risk the prince being killed instead of bothering him?"

Zeno would have understood if they'd been working for any other prince of Hell, but he'd spent time with Berith, albeit not a lot. The prince was nothing like what Zeno had heard about other princes of Hell, so the guard shouldn't be worried that he'd have them punished because they bothered him. He seemed to be a good prince, and they didn't have a reason not to help him when he was attacked.

"This won't happen again," she promised.

Berith threw the arm at her. She scrambled to catch it, her eyes wide as she looked down at it. "I sure hope it won't," Berith said. "It's happened too many times recently. You need to do your job. If you can't, I'll find someone else to do it for you."

"There won't be any need to do that," she said, her entire body tense. She held the arm gingerly, as if she expected it to attack her.

Now *that* would have been a sight.

Berith waved. "Go. Take these bodies with you and send someone to clean up the blood."

"Of course, your Majesty."

"And make sure to leave guards at the door, although I'm not worried we'll be attacked again. With Zeno here, even if we are, we'll be able to defend ourselves."

The prince looked at Zeno, who bowed his head slightly. He normally wouldn't, because he didn't care who was a prince and who wasn't, but Berith wasn't just a prince of Hell. He was Sabin's best friend, and that was more important to Zeno than the fact that he was a prince of Hell.

Zeno hovered close by as several guards came in to pick up the bodies. They were dragging them out, and blood was smeared all over the place.

"I have to say, it's a surprise to see you again," the prince said as he flopped onto one of the armchairs by the window. "Did you stay in the city?"

Zeno forced himself to step away from the bodies. Those demons were dead, and they weren't going to do anything. They certainly wouldn't attack Sabin again.

"No. I went into the desert and headed home, just like I said I would."

"Then how are you here?" Sabin asked, coming closer.

He held a hand as if he wanted to touch Zeno, but he didn't. Instead, he dropped it and stared at him. Zeno almost reached for him, but he could feel the prince's gaze on him, and he wasn't comfortable doing anything like that where the prince could see him. He wasn't sure he was comfortable taking Sabin's hand or touching him at all in front of anyone.

He cleared his throat, focusing on the prince's question rather than on Sabin. "When I stopped for the night, I heard people close by talking about the fact that they were going to attack the prince," he explained. "So I came back in a rush."

Sabin frowned. "Why didn't you kill them right away? Why did you come back to the palace?" His eyes widened. "Not that I'm not happy to see you, because I am. I'm just wondering."

Zeno wasn't offended, but he wasn't entirely sure how to answer the question. It would have been easier for him to dispatch the three demons in the desert and then go home. It was what most demons would have done, yet, he hadn't been able to. He'd been too worried about Sabin and something happening to him, and he'd been right, although he supposed that Sabin wouldn't have been attacked if he'd killed the demons when he'd first noticed them.

"I thought we could capture them and find out who was behind the plot, but I arrived too late."

The prince snorted. "I wasn't going to stop and ask them why they were here."

"I realize that now. I'm sorry I let them get so close to you."

The prince waved Zeno's words away. "It wasn't your responsibility to make sure we weren't attacked, and besides, you helped as soon as you got here. You saved Sabin, and that's the most important thing." He looked at Sabin. "But I was right."

Sabin glared at him. "And you're going to remind me of that forever, aren't you?"

The smile the prince gave Sabin was wicked. "How could I not? I told you that you needed protection, and you brushed me off."

"I'm not supposed to need protection in the palace. How do they keep sneaking in?" Sabin turned to Zeno. "Did you hear anything about that?"

"No. One of them said he knew someone in the palace who could let them in, but he was cagey. He didn't even tell his friends who that person was."

The prince sighed heavily. "I see. We're going to have to find out who that demon is soon. I can defend myself, but my daughter can't, and she's not the only one. In the meantime, Zeno, have you changed your mind about staying? No matter what Sabin says, he does need a bodyguard."

Zeno had no doubt about that. He wanted Sabin to be protected, and to his own surprise, he wanted to say yes and be the one to do that.

But nothing had changed. The palace still wasn't his home, and it still wasn't a place where he belonged. Was he ready to sacrifice his life and his comfort in order to save Sabin, or should he continue saying no? He knew which answer his heart wanted to give, but the problem was that his brain was pushing him to give a different one.

Chapter Eleven

Sabin watched Zeno pace in the garden just outside the office. He wasn't surprised that Zeno's answer to Berith's demand that he stay at the palace had been *no* again. He wasn't sure why Berith had felt he needed to ask a second time. Zeno was a demon who knew what he wanted and what he didn't want, and clearly, he didn't want to stay at the palace. It might be hard to understand for Sabin and Berith, but Sabin didn't want Zeno to do something he didn't feel he could do just because he was afraid for him.

"You should talk to him," Berith said.

Sabin turned to see that Berith was watching him the way he'd been watching Zeno. "And what am I supposed to tell him?"

"Why don't you explain that you like him and that you want him to stay so you can see where things go between the two of you?"

Sabin glared. He wasn't surprised Berith could read him so easily and precisely. "I can already imagine how that would go. I'd tell him I like him, and he'd look at me as if I'm nuts. He probably doesn't even understand what that means."

Berith cocked his head. "Why do you say that?"

Sabin sighed. "He has a reputation."

"Does he?"

There was something in Berith's tone that made Sabin narrow his eyes. "He does."

"And does that reputation mean he can't fall in love?"

"What are you hiding from me?" Because Berith was

hiding *something*.

"I wanted to see when you'd tell me who Zeno was, but you didn't. Were you planning on ever doing so?"

Sabin groaned and briefly closed his eyes. He tried to relax in his armchair, but he couldn't. Berith's words danced in his mind. "You know who he is."

"Of course I do. Did you really think I wouldn't recognize one of the most dangerous demons in my territory?"

Sabin opened his eyes to look at him. "How? I didn't recognize him when we first met. I traveled with him, and I didn't know who he was until we were almost attacked and those two demons apologized and ran away."

Berith barked out a laugh. "I'm not even surprised. He didn't tell you who he was right away?"

"He was afraid I'd be terrified and run." And he wouldn't have been wrong, but Sabin had gotten to know Zeno before finding out who he was, and he had a hard time putting those two personalities together.

He'd seen Zeno fight, and he'd seen him kill, but in Sabin's mind, Zeno was still the demon who'd saved him and brought him home. He'd made sure Sabin was fed, that his head was covered, and that he took breaks. That didn't match with Zeno's reputation as The Mercenary.

Berith leaned forward and patted Sabin's knee. "I'm not angry because you didn't tell me. I understand why you didn't."

"Do you?"

"I know you think I'm an idiot most of the time, and you might not be wrong, but I know you. You wanted me to give Zeno a chance, and you thought I wouldn't if I knew who he was. You're probably not wrong. It took me a few days to realize who he was, and when I did, he was already leaving. There was no point in telling him that I knew who he was."

"What will you do now?"

"Nothing. I offered him a job again, and he said no. I'll let him go, just like I did the first time." He grimaced. "But you really need to get a bodyguard. Even if you don't think you need protection, you could do it for me. I'd feel better if I knew you were protected like the rest of my family."

Sabin wanted to point out that Lon was very much part of their family, yet he didn't have to hang around with a bodyguard, but he didn't. Lon was head of security, and he knew how to defend himself as well as Berith. On the other hand, Sabin wouldn't be able to fight his way out of Mel's kindergarten class.

The kids would win.

Noise at the door made Sabin look up. He was thankful he didn't have to answer now, but he'd have to think about it. No matter how much he wanted Zeno to stay and protect him, that wasn't going to happen. He needed to face that fact and decide what would be best for him, and when it came to that, Berith was right. He needed a bodyguard because he might not make it out in one piece the next time he was attacked.

But he grinned when he saw Reyni walk in, his grumpy face twisted in a scowl. He was carrying his bag, and he peered at the blood on the floor. "Who did you kill this time?" he asked as he made his way toward the two of them.

Most demons wouldn't have dared talk to Berith that way, but Reyni didn't hesitate. He treated Berith as if he was just another demon, something Sabin knew Berith appreciated. That probably was why Reyni would get a promotion soon. Sabin wouldn't be surprised if he eventually became head of the palace healers.

"Just demons who attacked Sabin and me," Berith said.

Reyni dropped his bag next to Sabin. "I see. Well, I suppose I can't be angry if you did so to defend yourself."

"Would you be angry if I'd killed those demons for fun?" Berith sounded curious, and Sabin was, too.

He liked Reyni, and he wanted to get to know him better. He doubted the healer would want to become their friend, but it was good to be friendly with everyone at the palace.

"Only if you'd gotten hurt in the process. I don't care who you kill, but don't give me more work."

Berith laughed. "Aren't you paid to be my healer?"

"I am, and I'm ready to step in and help anytime you need me, your Majesty, but I'd appreciate it if you weren't an idiot and got yourself killed just because you can."

Berith was still grinning like the idiot Reyni clearly thought he was. "I can't promise I won't ever do anything stupid, but I'll try. I'm fine, but I need you to check over Sabin."

Sabin scowled, then turned his attention to Reyni. "They didn't even touch me, and I certainly didn't fight them. The one you need to check is Berith."

"I won't check either of you if you don't shut up. How about you tell me if anything hurts, and we go from there?"

Sabin nodded and forced himself to relax. Reyni would do his job whether he and Berith liked it or not, so they might as well lie back and allow him to poke at them.

"You don't think Zeno will stay," Berith said after a moment.

"He said no, not once, but twice. Why would you think he'd stay?"

Berith shrugged. "I don't know. I thought that maybe seeing that you were attacked would push him into staying."

"This isn't the first time someone's attacked me and he had to save me. It won't change anything."

"Pity. Maybe you could go with him?"

Sabin stared at him like he was an idiot. "And go where?"

"Wherever he lives."

"Can you imagine me living out there in the desert? I'd die in two days, and I'd only make it that far because Zeno would be with me." Sabin shook his head. "No. Just like this isn't Zeno's world, the desert isn't mine. I like him, but I can see that we're never going to work, and that's all right."

Sabin could feel Berith's gaze on him. It was heavy with

questions, but Sabin didn't want him to ask them. He didn't want to think about how he felt about Zeno leaving, either. It was hard enough without having to explain why it did.

"I still think you should put in more of an effort, both of you," Berith eventually said.

"Not everyone is as lucky as you. Mel was basically dumped into your lap, so you didn't have to make compromises to keep him."

"That's not true. I expected him to leave."

Sabin had expected Mel to leave, too. The human was delicate, and he didn't understand how demons lived. Well, he hadn't understood before. He was still horrified by the violence, but he wouldn't use it as an excuse to leave and go back to the human realm. Sabin was glad Mel had realized that he'd never be able to change how things worked in Hell and that Berith was more important than changing things. He was still doing what he could so that the next generation would be gentler, but while Hell wasn't his place, he was ready to sacrifice his life in the human realm for Berith.

Things were different for Sabin and Zeno. Sabin couldn't leave the palace. He had too many responsibilities, and he'd die in the desert. Zeno couldn't leave the desert because that was where he was more comfortable. There was no way anything could work between them, and Sabin almost wished Zeno hadn't come back.

Zeno kept an eye on Sabin from the garden. He'd noticed the same healer who'd examined Sabin when he'd first come home from the desert had arrived, and he felt that Sabin was safe enough that he didn't have to hover too close. He wanted to go to him, but he didn't want to be overwhelming, and besides, what would be the point? He'd said no to Berith's job offer again, so he wasn't staying. He shouldn't get too close to Sabin, although he suspected it was already too late.

No matter the distance between them, he'd always wonder if Sabin was okay. He could only imagine how he'd feel if something happened to Sabin, which was a definite possibility, considering how bad palace security was.

How could that be, when there were so many guards around? Their job was to protect the prince and his family, yet from what Zeno had been told, the prince had been attacked several times over the past few months.

But that wasn't Zeno's business. It couldn't be when he was trying to convince himself that his place was in the desert and that he needed to go. It would be better for Sabin, who'd be able to go back to his normal life without having Zeno hanging around like a dark cloud.

Zeno knew the kind of reaction he got from people. The only reason he'd been welcomed at the palace was that no one knew who he was. If they'd found out he was The Mercenary, he would have been kicked out — if he was lucky. He'd probably have been put to death if he wasn't, which wasn't something he wanted to consider.

He waited until the healer was busy with Sabin to walk into the office again. Berith had stood up to give Sabin and the healer some privacy, and he made a beeline for Zeno. Zeno didn't understand why the prince was so eager to talk to him, but he wasn't about to ask.

"I should head out," he said instead.

The prince frowned. "You're not thinking about leaving without saying goodbye to Sabin, are you?"

"Technically, we've already said goodbye."

The prince snorted. "And you think that's going to work with Sabin? If you do, you don't know him as well as I thought."

He wasn't wrong. If Zeno tried sneaking out without saying goodbye, Sabin would probably hunt him through the desert. "I just don't want to bother him. He's been through another attack, and he needs rest, not to be bothered by me."

"He wants to be bothered. Don't be a coward, Mercenary."

Zeno jerked back. He'd heard the word coming from the prince's mouth, but he had to be wrong. There was no way Berith would stand next to him, teasing him about being The Mercenary.

But Berith grinned, exposing his fangs. "Yes, I know who you are. Sabin might think I'm an idiot, but I guessed."

"When?"

"The day you decided to leave. I would have said something, but since you weren't staying, I didn't feel there was a need for me to."

"Why say something now?"

Berith shrugged. "Honestly, I'm not sure. I just know I wish you'd stay and protect Sabin. There's nothing I can do or say to convince you to do so?"

"I'm sorry, but no."

Berith nodded as if he expected this answer. "I understand."

"Do you?"

Berith looked toward the garden. His expression had changed, and he was almost wistful now. "Believe it or not, I do. Being a prince of Hell isn't always great. If I'm honest, it rarely is."

"Yet I don't think you'll ever step down from your throne."

"I can't. It would put my family in danger, and I won't allow that to happen. If it means I have to be a prince of Hell, then so be it."

Zeno could understand that, even though he didn't have a family. He would have done anything for his foster siblings when he was younger.

"Well, if you're not staying, at least go to the kitchens to get more food. It can be my personal thanks for saving Sabin's life again," Berith said with a smile.

Zeno wasn't going to say no to that. He still had food in his bag, but he'd eaten some on the road, so it would be good to get more. Before he headed there, he looked back at Sabin.

"He'll be safe," Berith promised. "I'll keep an eye on him, if it makes you feel better. You do realize that eventually, though, he won't be protected?"

Zeno glared at him. "You won't convince me to change my mind."

Berith raised his hands. "I had to try. But I understand not wanting to do something, so I'll stop pushing."

He also understood doing something because it was the best for the people he loved. It was a surprise, but Zeno tried not to think too much about it. He wasn't in love with Sabin. He didn't owe Sabin anything more than he'd already done.

Or at least, that was what he tried convincing himself of on his way to the kitchens.

He'd only been there once, but he remembered the way without having to ask. That was good, because he didn't fancy stopping demons in the middle of the hallway to ask where the kitchens were. He didn't want to talk to demons and risk that one of them would recognize him. The prince had nothing to say about his presence at the palace, but other demons might protest, and Zeno didn't want to be kicked out before he had a chance to say goodbye to Sabin.

No matter what he'd said about already having done so, it would give him one last opportunity to spend time with Sabin, and that was something he wanted to take advantage of.

He walked into the wide kitchens with purpose. Just like the last time he'd been here, the air smelled both salty and sweet at the same time. Cooks were running around, getting food ready for lunch and snacks for the children the prince's consort taught. An enormous cake was on one table, possibly for dinner.

And sitting at a table in the corner was a human.

Zeno had met him before, so he recognized Mel, the prince's consort. They hadn't really talked, and he wouldn't know what to say to him, so he kept his distance and moved toward the cooks. He explained why he was there, and they were more than happy to fill his bag with food again.

When he turned around, it was to find the human looking at him. When they made eye contact, Mel smiled and gestured at him to come to sit at his table. Zeno wished he could say no, because he didn't know how to behave with humans, but this wasn't just any human. He wasn't about to risk the prince's wrath because he didn't want to chat.

So, while the cooks were filling his bag, Zeno made his way toward the table. There was an empty cup in front of the human, and he was reading something on a tablet. He put it down when he realized Zeno would talk to him, and he smiled.

Zeno had thought the human cute before, but now he could see how truly beautiful he was. It wasn't just because to a demon, he was odd-looking. He had a gentle smile and kind eyes, and Zeno understood why the man was a teacher.

"I didn't expect to see you again. I thought you'd left."

Zeno wasn't sure what he should tell the human. He'd no doubt find out that Berith had been attacked soon enough, but did Zeno want to be the one to tell him about it?

He cleared his throat. "I heard demons were planning to attack the prince, so I came back."

"You wanted to save Berith?"

"Yes." Zeno wasn't going to say anything about the prince being attacked. The prince could tell his consort himself.

"Thank you. I know you were eager to get back to the desert."

"I was, but I could protect the prince."

"I'm sure he's not the only one you wanted to protect."

So the human could see right through Zeno, too. Zeno had to be more careful. "I wished to make sure Sabin was all right, too," he admitted.

"You know, you could stay with us."

"This isn't my home."

"It wasn't mine, either. I made it my home, and it is so because of the people who live here, not because of the place it is."

The words went straight through Zeno's heart. Mel wasn't wrong. Hell wasn't his place, yet he'd built a home here with the people he loved.

Why couldn't Zeno do the same?

"I'm assigning Roque and Yatim to your protection," Berith declared.

"You can't," Sabin protested. "They're the best, and you need to keep them with Mel."

"Mel is protected enough. He's always around other demons, and even if they're not fighters, they can step in to help if he needs them to. On the other hand, you spend a lot of time on your own, either in your office, in your rooms, or in the garden."

"There are other guards. I can take them rather than Mel's bodyguards."

Berith's eyes narrowed. "You do realize that I'm the prince and that you're supposed to listen to me, right?"

Sabin resisted the urge to stick his tongue out, because he wasn't a child, but he was tempted. "I know you're the boss, *your Majesty*. It doesn't mean I don't think you're making a mistake by assigning me your consort's bodyguards."

"Don't be mouthy. I'm just worried about what's going to happen once you get back on the road."

Sabin's brain screeched to a halt. "I'm sorry?"

"You have to finish the trip. You insisted that it was a necessity, and I agree."

Sabin shot to his feet. Thankfully, Reyni had left, muttering about how stupid Sabin and Berith were. Sabin couldn't say he disagreed. "I need to call Reyni back," he said.

Berith frowned. "Why? Are you hurt?"

"I'm not, but *you* will be once I'm done kicking your ass. I can't believe you think I'm going back on the road after what happened to me the last time I was there. How can you ask this of me?"

Sabin started pacing the office. It was true that he'd insisted this trip was necessary, and he still thought it was. It had been interrupted, but they needed to finish talking to Berith's vassals. If they didn't, the demons might move on to another prince and swap loyalties, which wasn't something they could afford.

But there was no way Sabin was going back to the desert.

"We don't have a choice," Berith said softly. "We have to finish this trip, and I can't come."

"Of course you can. You're the prince. This is *your* responsibility."

"But I'm not leaving my family when I know there's someone in the palace who wants all of them to die," Berith snapped.

Sabin stared at him. He couldn't remember the last time Berith had been angry at him. Even now, he didn't think it was true. It sounded more like Berith was frustrated because he wanted to protect both his family and Sabin, but he couldn't. Someone had to go on the road and represent him, and it could only be someone he trusted implicitly.

The most logical someone was Sabin.

A knock on the door made both of them jump. It opened, and Mel's head poked through. He was frowning, and when he saw it was only Berith and Sabin in the room, he made a beeline for the prince.

"What's going on? We heard yelling."

Zeno was right behind Mel. He was holding his bag, which was so full of food it looked like it was about to burst. He looked from the prince to Sabin, a frown on his beautiful face.

Sabin was glad he'd been keeping the hood down. It made Zeno uncomfortable, but it was less conspicuous in the palace.

It also gave Sabin the opportunity to look at him, something he wouldn't have for long.

"What's going on?" Mel asked.

Berith rubbed his face. "I was telling Sabin that someone needs to finish the trip. It can't be me, because I won't leave you and the others on your own when someone is actively trying to hurt my family. But Sabin doesn't want to go back to the desert, and I don't blame him. I just don't see another solution."

"You're sending him back?" Zeno said with a growl.

"Not because I want to, but because I have to. I don't know how much you know about all of this, but if I don't keep my vassals happy, they'll betray me. That would put everyone in danger, including Sabin. That means we have to finish this trip and talk to everyone who wants to talk to us, but I can't be the one who does it. I'm not leaving Mel and my daughter here on their own."

Sabin understood where Berith was coming from. He'd been angry at first, and he still was, but not at Berith. His friend was between a rock and a hard place, and he was trying to find a way to keep everyone safe. Unfortunately, it meant someone would have to sacrifice themselves, and it looked like that person would be Sabin.

"Zeno, what do you think?" Mel asked.

Sabin blinked at the easy way Mel talked to Zeno. He'd expected Mel to be afraid of Zeno, but maybe he didn't know who Zeno was. Even if he did, Sabin doubted that the name The Mercenary would mean anything to him. He lived in Hell, but he was sheltered here at the palace. He wouldn't know anything about what Zeno did on a regular basis.

"I have no idea how any of this works," Zeno said. "But if Sabin has to go back on the road, he should be well protected this time."

"That's the problem," Berith said. "I thought he was well protected the last time, but all the guards died."

"They tried protecting me. They were just outnumbered," Sabin murmured.

Sometimes, he still thought about those guards. He hadn't been close to any of them, but it didn't mean he'd wanted them to die. He hated that they'd sacrificed their lives to save his, even though it was their job. Knowing that it had wouldn't make things easier for the families those guards had left behind.

"I'll think about a better way to do this, but I don't know if I can come up with anything," Berith said.

Sabin regretted the way he'd snapped at his friend. It had been a knee-jerk reaction because he didn't want to go back into the desert, but Berith was right. Someone needed to finish this job, and it wouldn't be him.

"I'll be staying around for a few days," Zeno said gruffly.

Sabin blinked at him. "Why? I expected you to want to leave right away." He peered at the bag Zeno was still holding. "You packed like you were going to."

"That was the plan, but now that I know about this, I want to stick around a bit longer."

"You don't have to. I'll be fine." The last thing Sabin wanted was for Zeno to be forced to stay when he didn't want to. He didn't want Zeno to resent him for anything or leave with bad memories of how things had gone between them.

"I'm staying, and that's final," Zeno said.

"I'm glad," Mel exclaimed.

Sabin eyed him. If someone had told him the consort would become friends with Zeno when he'd first met The Mercenary, he would have thought they were nuts. He could see it, though. Zeno was quiet, but Mel often talked enough for two people. He was gentle, but that didn't mean he wasn't strong, and he could see through most people. No matter how angry and dangerous they appeared, Mel knew when they were good people.

Clearly, he thought that was the case with Zeno. Sabin

couldn't say he disagreed, even though he didn't know what to make of Zeno's decision to stick around.

Chapter Twelve

Sabin glared at the two bodyguards following him down the hallway. Yatim stared back while Roque gave him a wide smile.

The asshole.

They'd started following him around when he'd left Berith's office yesterday after they'd been attacked. He'd done everything he could to get them to leave, but they took their orders directly from the prince, which meant they were glued to Sabin's ass.

And Sabin hated it.

He wasn't used to needing bodyguards, and he didn't know what to do with them. He felt awkward and like he needed to act unnaturally, and that wasn't something he enjoyed when he was in his home.

Of course, he also wouldn't enjoy being attacked, but still. He was convinced he didn't need bodyguards, and he wanted to convince the prince of that, even though it was pointless to try. When Berith got an idea, he followed it until the end.

Besides, there was a trip to think about. As much as Sabin didn't want to leave the palace again, he was going to have to. Many demons were waiting to speak with a representative of Berith, and that representative would be Sabin. He just wanted to convince Berith that he didn't need Roque and Yatim to come with him and that they'd be better off keeping an eye on Mel.

He stormed into the dining room, ready for dinner. He wasn't surprised to see everyone was already there until his gaze stopped on Zeno.

Now *that* was a surprise.

Zeno looked extremely uncomfortable. He'd been given clothes that didn't look out of place in the palace but clearly didn't belong on him. Whoever had chosen them for him had stayed simple, but they were still more ornate than what Zeno had been wearing when he and Sabin met. There was no hood on the shirt, which meant he was exposed to anyone who wished to look at him. Right now, it was only family and friends in the dining room, but Sabin could guess how Zeno had to feel, and he was sorry for him. Maybe he should try to convince Zeno to leave soon. There was no point in him staying, anyway.

Sabin plopped into his chair and glared at Berith. "Do they really have to follow me everywhere I go?" he asked, gesturing at Roark and Yatim, who'd entered the dining room after him and now stood against the wall behind him.

Berith grinned. "That's kind of the point of having bodyguards."

Something in his smile told Sabin he wasn't done and that he was planning something. That never ended well, especially for Sabin.

"They're nice," Mel said. "I like both of them."

"I never said they weren't nice, but I don't need them to follow me around the palace."

"I think you do, especially after you and Berith were recently attacked." He glared at Berith. "Although I wouldn't know about *that* if I hadn't heard the gossip."

Sabin grinned at Berith. He wasn't sure what his friend had been thinking, trying to hide the most recent attack from Mel, but he should have expected his consort to find out. From what Sabin knew, the screaming could be heard on the other side of the palace. Mel had scolded Berith in a way no one else dared do, and that made Sabin happy.

"Well, I'm sure we can find another solution if you don't

want Roque and Yatim to come with you. Maybe Zeno could be your bodyguard for the trip?" Berith asked.

Sabin grabbed the knife by his plate. He was tempted to throw it at Berith's face, but instead, he wrapped his fingers around it. "What are you talking about?"

"You'll go back on the road soon, and you'll have to travel through the desert. That's kind of Zeno's home, isn't it?"

"Even if it is, it's not his job to protect me. He's already done more than enough for me, and we can't impose on him."

"I don't think it would be imposing. Since he saved you twice, surely, it means he wants you to stay alive. I'm sure he's worried about what you'll be up to in the desert on your own."

Sabin pointed the knife at Berith. "You're talking as if you're planning on sending me there on my own, but that's not so."

"Of course not. You'll be given plenty of guards. Since a dozen wasn't enough, I'm thinking of multiplying that number. How about thirty?"

Sabin shuddered at the thought. It had been hard enough for him to travel with twelve bodyguards, and he didn't want to think about what it'd be like if he had to deal with thirty of them. "Surely, there's another way."

"Like I said, Zeno could protect you. He knows the desert better than anyone, and considering most demons are terrified of him, they'll think twice about trying to attack you."

"Why are most demons terrified of him?" Mel asked.

So Berith hadn't told him about Zeno's reputation. That was good, because Sabin didn't want him to be afraid of Zeno. To everyone's surprise, the two of them seemed to have become friends, and Sabin wanted that to continue. He wanted Zeno to see that not everyone was afraid of him and that if he wanted, he could have a nice life here at the palace.

Yes, he still had hope that Zeno would decide to stay with him. He was aware that it was stupid and pointless, but he couldn't do anything about how he felt. What he *could* do something about was Berith's plan.

"No."

Berith blinked. "What do you mean?"

"I won't force Zeno to come with us. He's headed home, and that's where he'll go."

"I don't think he'll want to. I'm sure he's worried about you getting attacked again."

"Then I'll have to make sure I'm not. I'll find a way to make this work."

"But *I'd* feel better if I knew you were well protected. There's no one I trust more with your safety than Zeno."

Sabin had no idea what to make of those words. "It doesn't make sense. You barely know him."

"I know enough of him to be sure you'd be safe with him."

That much was true, but could Sabin ask Zeno to do this? "You could always send someone else," he tried. "Maybe one of your ministers."

"Everyone knows you're my right-hand man. They'd be offended if I sent anyone but you in my place."

Sabin groaned and buried his face in his hands. "Why do you have to be right about this?" he whined.

"Because I'm right about everything. Face it, Sabin. You're going back on the road, and you're doing it well protected."

Sabin supposed it could have been worse. He wasn't looking forward to traveling through the desert again, but at least Berith wasn't sending him out there with only one guard.

Zeno tried his best not to laugh, but the friendship between Sabin and the prince amused him. He doubted most people could talk like that to Berith and keep their heads, but Sabin didn't have a problem with it. Everyone around the table acted as if this was normal, so Zeno suspected it was.

His thoughts went to what Berith had said. He understood

the reasoning behind having to get Sabin back on the road, but he was worried. It had been a disaster the first time around. What were the odds it wouldn't be the second time? The thought of Sabin walking around in the desert on his own made Zeno shudder in horror. He couldn't let that happen, but what could he do to stop it?

It was obvious that whatever he said, Sabin would get back on the road. He might not want to, but he'd have to. Berith had promised he'd give Sabin more guards than he had the first time around, but would they be enough?

Zeno knew the desert. He knew how dangerous it was, which areas it was best to stay away from, and which to stick to. He knew who to avoid and who would welcome Sabin as the prince's representative. He couldn't work miracles, so there was still a possibility Sabin might be attacked, but if he was, it would be easy for Zeno to step in.

But all of that meant that Zeno would have to go with Sabin.

Was that something Zeno wanted to do? He'd said no when the prince had offered him a job as Sabin's bodyguard, but that had been when he'd thought he'd have to stay at the palace. He couldn't live the rest of his life surrounded by people who stared at him, and he couldn't share his living space with so many other people he didn't trust. He was sure the servants meant well — although considering one of them let in demons who tried killing the prince, maybe that wasn't the case — but he couldn't live here.

But maybe he could be Sabin's bodyguard in the desert. He could stay with him for his trip, make sure he came home in one piece, and only then leave. He was sure Berith would pay him whatever he asked for, and it wasn't like he had anything or anyone waiting for him at home. His shack would still be standing by the time this was over — possibly.

Decision made, he cleared his throat. It took a moment for the people around the table to realize he wanted to say something and even longer for everyone to shut up. Berith and Sabin were still poking fun at each other and, at the same time, trying to find a way to make this trip work.

"Will you shut up?" Mel asked, poking a finger into Berith's side. "Zeno is trying to say something."

"I like your hair," the little girl who'd been introduced to Zeno as Berith's daughter said. She was sitting on the other side of the table, quite far from Zeno, but he'd noticed her staring.

He had no idea how to behave with children, so he gave her a tight smile. "Thank you. I like your hair, too."

She beamed and touched it. "Mel did it for me."

Zeno nodded. What could he say to that?

But now he had everyone's attention. They were all staring at him, which was another thing he hated. It was easy enough to focus on Sabin, though, so that was what he did. He turned and looked at the demon sitting next to him, and when he did, he knew he'd made the right decision. Sabin deserved to be protected, and that was what Zeno would do.

"Since it looks like nothing will change the fact that you have to get back on the road, I decided to accept Berith's job offer," he said.

Sabin frowned and put down his fork. "Which one?"

"I'll come with you and be your bodyguard while you're on the road. I know the desert, and I know where we'll be welcome and where we won't. As you've seen, I can defend you from a number of dangers, so I'm more than capable of keeping you safe."

"I'll pay you whatever you want," Berith declared. When Zeno looked at him, he raised his wineglass to him.

"I'm not doing this for the money," Zeno told him.

"Maybe not, but it's still a job, and I intend on paying you. I pay Mel for his work as a teacher. This isn't any different."

Zeno was surprised to find out that the prince paid his consort, but maybe he shouldn't be. Things were very different here at the palace from how they were in the rest of Hell, and it was as surprising as it was intriguing.

"Just take what he's offering," Sabin murmured. "You've lifted a huge weight off his shoulders by accepting to come with me. If you don't tell him how much you want to be paid, he'll try to shower you with gold and whatever else he can stick in there."

"I don't need much. I'm okay being paid whatever one of the guards at the palace gets paid."

Berith tsked. "You'll be Sabin's personal bodyguard. That means you'll get more, and I don't want to hear no for an answer. I'm your prince."

He wasn't wrong about that. Zeno might live in the middle of nowhere, but he was still in Berith's territory. It was vast, and he doubted he'd ever have met the prince if he hadn't saved Sabin, but technically, he was supposed to obey Berith.

"You don't have to do it if you don't feel up to it," Sabin whispered. He was clearly trying to talk to Zeno without the others hearing what he was saying, but it wasn't working. Everyone around the table was staring at them.

"I wouldn't be saying yes to this if I wasn't sure. I don't want anything to happen to you, especially not after I worked so hard to get you home in one piece."

Sabin chuckled and poked at something on his plate with his fork. He hadn't eaten much, and Zeno found himself worried about that. If they were going to be traveling, Sabin needed his strength, especially after what he'd already gone through in the desert. He needed to eat, sleep, and rest as much as possible before they left.

"Well, at least this trip won't be such a disaster," Sabin eventually said. He turned and smiled at Zeno. "I was worried about what would happen to me if I was on my own, so I'm glad to find out I won't be."

"You wouldn't have been even if Zeno hadn't said yes," the prince pointed out. "You make me sound like a cruel asshole who would have sent you on your own in the desert, on foot and without food."

Zeno didn't point out that the guards the prince had sent Sabin off with the first time around hadn't been much help. It wasn't their fault, and they'd died for their inability to keep Sabin safe. That was the problem with these palace people. They had no idea how life was out there in the desert, and they paid for it when they tried exploring it. That was probably why they usually kept to their palaces, but since Sabin wasn't going to, Zeno would make sure he was safe.

"Thank you," Sabin said.

"Thank me once we're back here and you're safe. This might be a disaster."

Sabin's smile was gentle. "Maybe, but at least I'll be with you. As far as I'm concerned, it'll be the best trip of my life.

"It'll only be the second trip you've gone on," the prince pointed out.

Sabin threw his fork at him.

Everyone around the table laughed, even Cyarea, who couldn't possibly understand why she was laughing. The tension loosened, as did Sabin. Zeno was still worried, though. He knew what to expect in the desert and how to survive, but the same couldn't be said for Sabin and the guards. If he was going to be on this trip and keep Sabin safe, he'd have to organize things the way he knew would be better. He'd probably step on some toes as he did so, but he didn't care. His job was to keep Sabin safe and bring him back to the palace, and that was what he'd do, even if it killed him.

Although he hoped it wouldn't.

CHAPTER THIRTEEN

Sabin looked around his room. He wasn't happy about leaving it again, but at least this time, he knew he'd be coming back. He'd been worried the first time Berith had sent him into the desert, and he'd been right. He'd almost died out there, and he would have if Zeno hadn't found him. Now, Zeno would be by his side, and it made Sabin feel better.

He still hated the thought of having to travel through the desert, though. He doubted anything would ever change his mind about that, which was one of the reasons he knew nothing could happen between him and Zeno. The desert was Zeno's home, while it was the last place Sabin wanted to spend time. How could anyone believe they could work as a couple?

A knock on the door made him turn. He hoped he'd packed everything he'd need on this trip, because it looked like he'd run out of time. He wasn't entirely sure he'd succeeded, but as it was, Zeno had already bitched that the cart Sabin intended to travel in would slow them down. Sabin had been glad when Berith had said it didn't matter and that the people they were visiting expected Sabin to travel like his representative, not like a demon who was just walking through Hell. Sabin already had enough of walking during his first trip in the desert, thank you very much.

"Yes?" he called out.

The door opened, and Lon peeked in. He looked around the bedroom, saw Sabin was on his own, and stepped in. "What are you doing?"

"Making sure I have everything I'll need." If he could, he'd bring his bathtub along.

"I still think this is a terrible idea," he said.

"And you think I don't? Trust me, if I could avoid this, I would. We know that's not possible, though, so please, stop obsessing over it."

Lon raised his hands. "All right. I apologize."

Sabin waved him away. "It's fine. I'm just nervous about traveling through the desert again."

"Anyone would be, considering what happened to you the last time. Zeno will keep you safe, though." He hesitated. "Berith told me who Zeno is."

Sabin wasn't surprised. "What do you think about it?"

Lon scowled. "I wish one of you had said something to me sooner. I'm the head of the palace security. I can't have The Mercenary hanging around without knowing he's there."

"It's not like he was doing anything wrong."

"Still. He has a reputation."

Sabin grinned. "What have you heard about him?" He liked talking about Zeno. Sometimes he felt like he'd never stop if he could, which was ridiculous. He wasn't a youngling with a crush on someone, dammit. He was an adult, and he was going on a dangerous trip that could mean his death. He needed to be careful, not moon over Zeno.

But he liked mooning over Zeno.

"Enough to know you'll be safe with him as long as he doesn't decide to kill you."

"He won't kill me. He has a code, and he sticks to it."

Lon snorted. "The Mercenary has a code. Who would've thought?"

"Well, think about the people we believe he killed. What do they have in common?"

"Apart from the fact that they died at his hand?"

"Most of them were assholes. We can't be entirely sure who he killed and didn't kill without asking him, but when he told me who he was, he explained that he never kills innocent demons. When someone hires him to do a job, he looks into the target and only then decides whether or not he'll take the job. He doesn't kill just anyone, Lon. I'll be fine as long as no one hires him to kill me."

Lon's eyes narrowed. "What if someone does try to hire him to kill you, then?"

Sabin's chest tightened, but he ignored it. "Even if someone tries to hire him, it won't change anything. Besides, why would someone want to kill me?"

"Maybe because of how close you are to Berith? Maybe because you're his representative, and killing you would make him look weak?"

"I already told you that Zeno doesn't kill innocents."

"And you qualify as an innocent?"

"I don't know. Maybe I don't because I've done things I'm not proud of, but I've never killed anyone, and I always do my best not to hurt people. When we talked about it before, Zeno said he'd never hurt me because he doesn't believe I deserve it, and I believe him." Sabin rubbed his face. He was already tired, and they weren't even on the road yet. "Look, you can keep worrying that he's going to kill me, or you can trust him and believe that he'll have my back and protect me. Are you going to worry the entire time I'm not home? That's why Berith wanted to hire Zeno—so he wouldn't have to worry."

Lon sighed, and his shoulders slumped. "I don't believe he'll hurt you," he said. "But I still dislike the thought of you in the desert. No matter who you're with, we all know how it ended up last time, and I don't like it."

"Trust me. I don't like it either. I wouldn't go if I didn't have to, but no matter how many times I tried to get out of it, I couldn't. I'd have insisted that Berith do this in any other circumstance, but I understand why he doesn't want to leave the palace. With the demons attacking and sneaking into the private wing, he needs to keep an eye on Mel and the rest of the family. He wouldn't be able to do that if he were on the road, which is why it makes sense that I'm the one to go."

"I know. That doesn't mean I have to like it."

Sabin knew how frustrated Lon was that he wasn't able to find out who kept letting in demons who tried killing the prince. He was head of security, and he should have that under control, but instead, he kept running into walls. Every time he thought he'd found the person who let the demons in, more demons snuck into the palace, and he had to start from the beginning again.

Lon, Sabin, and Berith worked together, but first and foremost, they were friends. It wasn't just that Lon felt he was failing as head of security. He also felt he was failing as a friend who was supposed to protect Berith and his family. He'd never forgive himself if something happened to any of them, and Sabin couldn't blame him. He wished he could do more to help him, but they each had their responsibilities and their own job.

Sabin moved closer and patted Lon's shoulder. "I can't promise everything will be all right, but I have a better chance of making it back alive than I did the first time around. Zeno won't let anything happen to me. I'm sure of that."

Lon stared at him for a moment before nodding. "I don't believe he will. He really likes you."

Sabin groaned. "Please don't start."

Lon relaxed, and Sabin was glad to hear him laugh. Things would turn serious again for both of them within minutes. They could afford to take just a moment to breathe.

"I'm just saying that Berith isn't the only one who noticed something is happening between you and Zeno," Lon explained.

"Nothing's happening between us," Sabin protested. "We became close while we were on the road, but that was to be expected."

"I don't think he'd have agreed to do this if he didn't care about you."

"Even if he does care about me, and I'm not saying he does, nothing will happen."

"Why not? If you like Zeno, and he likes you, I don't see a reason the two of you shouldn't be together. We thought things would never work between Berith and Mel, yet they're happy together. Love has a way of making things work, even when you don't believe they can."

Sabin pointed his finger at his friend. "Who talked about love?"

"What have we been talking about the entire time? You have a crush on Zeno, at the very least."

"I do, but it doesn't mean I'm in love with him. It also doesn't mean he's in love with me, but even if we were madly in love, it still can't work. He's a desert demon. I'm bitching about being away from the palace. How do you think we could find common ground?"

"I'm sure you'll find a way."

Sabin wished Lon was right, but he doubted it. He already knew how things would go. He and Zeno would travel together, and he'd fall even more in love with Zeno during the trip. Eventually, though, the trip would end, and Zeno would bring Sabin home. Once he did, he'd head out into the desert again, leaving Sabin behind.

Sabin needed to guard his heart and make sure he didn't fall even more in love with Zeno, but he wasn't sure how to make that happen. He was already more than halfway there.

No matter how hard he guarded his heart, disappointment and pain were on the horizon.

Zeno glared at the carts. Were they essential? Sabin could walk like the rest of them, and as for the food and drinks, they could each carry whatever they needed, right? That was what Sabin and Zeno had done on their way to the palace, and Zeno didn't fully understand why this time had to be different.

"You look like you're planning to kill someone," Berith said from beside him.

Zeno turned to look at the prince. "I just don't understand why we need all that stuff."

"I realize it would be faster and easier for you to travel lighter, but you have to behave as if Sabin is me. If I were traveling, I wouldn't be walking around carrying food and water. I'd be sitting in the cart, letting other people do the hard work for me. It's what demons expect from a prince, and they might not take it well if they don't get it."

And Berith couldn't afford to lose anyone's loyalty, but especially not the loyalty of some of the demons Sabin would be visiting.

Zeno sighed. "All of this is really fucking complicated."

Berith laughed and clapped Zeno's shoulder. "I can't say I disagree. Unfortunately, there's nothing I can do to change it. You're already traveling much lighter than I would if I were going instead of Sabin. It wouldn't look good if I allowed my right-hand man to travel on foot with barely enough water and food."

Besides, Sabin would be more comfortable like this. In the end, that was all that mattered to Zeno. He wasn't doing this because he wanted to do a favor for Berith. He was going along with this mess because he wanted to make sure Sabin was safe, and that was what he'd focus on. It wouldn't be anything like what he was used to when it came to traveling through the desert, but he could do it anyway.

He had to.

"There's Sabin," Berith said.

Zeno looked up to see Sabin coming out of the palace, Lon walking beside him. They were talking, and from the smile on their faces, it wasn't anything bad. Sabin, Lon, and Berith were longtime friends, and that mattered more to them than their jobs. Sabin would no doubt miss his family and friends, and it was Zeno's job to make sure he made it back in one piece so he could spend time with them again.

"Ready?" Sabin asked when he reached Zeno.

"As ready as we can be," Zeno confirmed.

Sabin looked around. "I suppose it's time to go, then."

Zeno took a step back to give Sabin the opportunity to say goodbye to his friends and family. Mel, Cyarea, and Cyarea's mother were there, and they all took a turn hugging Sabin. It was as if they didn't believe he'd come back, no matter what Zeno promised. He understood where they were coming from. The desert was a dangerous place, and Sabin had already been there, had run for his life, and had made it back to the palace. He'd do it again. Zeno would make sure of it.

After Cyarea had hugged Sabin three times, Sabin finally stepped toward the cart. He stared at his family, almost as if he couldn't look away, but Zeno caught his gaze. He smiled and nodded, and he finally climbed into the cart.

Zeno relaxed. They were a little late already, but it didn't matter.

Sabin had given him his itinerary, so he knew where they were going. Sabin had already visited the first two towns the first time he'd been on the road, so they'd be skipping those and going straight to the next one. From there, they could follow Sabin's initial plan. Zeno had made a few changes, and he'd been tempted to make more when he'd seen where they'd have to travel, but he hadn't. If visiting the place where he'd spent his childhood was a problem, he'd tell Sabin about it once they got there.

"Keep him safe," Berith said next to Zeno.

Zeno nodded. "That's what you pay me for."

To Zeno's astonishment, Berith pulled him into his arms and hugged him. It was shorter than the hug he'd given Sabin, but it told everyone around them that Zeno was a close friend of the prince, too. Zeno hadn't expected that, and he wasn't quite sure what to make of it, so he limited himself to patting the prince's back as they both retreated.

"We'll see you soon," Berith said.

Zeno could only nod. He *hoped* they'd see him soon. If they didn't, it would mean he'd failed.

He looked at the group of guards standing by the carts. He found the one in charge, and when he nodded, she turned to the other guards. A few words from her, and the carts moved forward. They were each pulled by two nuckelavee, and while Zeno had no idea how to deal with the demonic horses, he wouldn't be the one taking care of them. That was a relief. He'd have enough work as it was keeping an eye on Sabin.

They started down the road, and Zeno walked next to Sabin's cart. Sabin kept peeking at him, but he stayed silent as they crossed the city. Children ran around the carts, waving and screaming at Sabin. He waved back, looking happy as a clam. That would change once they reached the desert, so Zeno let him. He doubted anyone in the crowd would try to attack him anyway.

Zeno had gathered that Berith and his family were well-liked in the city. Even though Berith was a prince of Hell, he was as fair as possible while also not letting anyone walk all over him. He was harsh when he needed to be and didn't hesitate to punish his enemies, but the city prospered, and everyone knew it was thanks to him. It had been a surprise to realize this because of how many demons had snuck into the palace to attack the prince, but Zeno supposed they could be sent by Berith's enemies. If Lon didn't manage to find out who was behind it by the time Zeno and Sabin came back, Zeno would poke around and see if maybe he could.

He relaxed once they were out of the city. It was easier to keep an eye on Sabin with fewer people around.

They walked for a while. Zeno was home in the desert, and he knew how to behave. The same couldn't be said of the palace, and he'd been tense the entire time he'd been there. Now, even though there was always a chance they could be attacked, it was easier to breathe.

At least until Sabin gestured at the guards guiding the nuckelavee. They stopped, and Sabin climbed out of the cart.

"What are you doing?" Zeno asked.

Sabin grinned at him. "This reminds me of the other time we were on the road together."

"It hasn't been that long. Besides, I doubt you have fond memories of that time."

"Actually, I do. If it hadn't been for the whole being attacked thing, I think I'd have liked spending time with you on the road. Even though I wasn't looking forward to this trip, I don't hate the idea as much now that I know you'll be with me."

Zeno was stunned by the admission. He'd known Sabin liked him, but now, it shone through every one of Sabin's words. Zeno didn't know what to say, or even if he should say something. He didn't want to make Sabin self-conscious, but he had no idea how to behave in this kind of situation.

He nodded. "You still should stay in the cart. It'll be easier on you."

"I can walk for a while. I won't be forced to walk the entire trip this time around, so I'm fine. I promise."

Zeno wanted to insist, but Sabin knew his body better than he did. He'd stop when he was too tired to continue walking. "All right. Keep an eye on the road and watch where you put your hooves."

"I will."

They started walking again, more slowly this time. No matter what Sabin said, Zeno didn't want him to get too tired. He had no idea what would be expected of them once they reached the first town they were headed to, but he suspected Sabin would have to meet and talk to people. He'd need to be rested for that, which meant Zeno would have to make sure that eventually he climbed back into the cart.

"So, what did you think of the palace?" Sabin asked.

Zeno wasn't used to chatting while he was on the road. He'd missed listening to Sabin talking about whatever crossed his mind, though, and he settled into the already familiar sensation with a smile.

He still wasn't sure what to think of this trip or if he'd made the right choice by coming, but at least it would give him the opportunity to spend more time with Sabin.

CHAPTER FOURTEEN

Sabin was exhausted, and he could have cried when they finally reached the first town a few days later. He'd walked most of the way, even though Zeno tried convincing him to climb back into the cart. He wanted Zeno to see that he was strong and that he'd be fine even on his own.

Of course, that probably wasn't correct. Even if Sabin could walk around the desert, there was a good chance that he'd already have been attacked if he were on his own. They'd seen people in the distance during the night, but thankfully, no one had come close. They probably would have if there hadn't been so many guards, and having them and Zeno with him made Sabin feel better.

They'd stopped a while back so that Sabin could wash up and climb back into the cart. He'd done his best to look good, since he was Berith's representative, but it wasn't easy when one was in the desert. Hopefully, he wouldn't put Berith to shame.

"You look good," Zeno murmured as they walked into the small town.

Sabin patted his hair. "Not too much dust?"

"As much dust as can be expected, considering you traveled through the desert. No one will care."

Sabin hoped so. Zeno knew these people better than Sabin could ever hope to, so he decided to trust him. Besides, it wasn't like he had a choice.

The guards guided the carts through town until they reached the biggest house. This was a small town, but lots of people were around, staring at him and murmuring to each other. Silence fell when the door of the house opened and a tall demon came out. His horns almost brushed the upper frame of the door, but he managed to get out without a problem. He grinned as if he were Sabin's long-lost friend and was happy to see him, and he walked toward the carts.

"Welcome, welcome," he declared.

He and the other vassals responsible for whatever towns Sabin would travel through had been warned that he was coming. They expected him, which Sabin hoped meant that this guy had food ready. Possibly a bath, too, although Sabin supposed he could do without.

He scrambled out of the cart. He was pretty sure he wasn't as graceful as he ought to be, but Zeno was there, holding out a hand to help him climb out. Sabin did so. Then, once his hooves were on the ground, he smoothed down his clothes. By the time he was done, the demon had reached them.

"As I'm sure you know, I'm Ysmal. Welcome to my small town." His voice boomed, making Sabin wince. After spending time in the desert, it was odd to have so many people talking around him.

Sabin plastered a smile on his lips. "Thank you for welcoming us."

"Of course. I can't wait to have a good chat with you, but I'm sure you and your guards will want a bit of rest, food, and the opportunity to clean up. I can only imagine how harsh the desert was on you."

Sabin could have kissed him. "It would be good to be able to clean up, at the very least," he confirmed.

"Good. You'll be staying the night at my home. The guards will be housed in other residences close by. I hope that's all right?"

Sabin looked at Zeno. He was the one who needed to decide if that was okay. While they were on the road, he was Sabin's head of security.

"It's fine if the guards are settled wherever you have space for them," he said. "But I'll be staying with Sabin."

"I assure you that no one here wants to hurt him."

"I'm sure that's true, but you have to understand the prince himself asked me to protect him."

"Of course. Well, you're welcome to share the bedroom. I'm afraid I don't have a second bedroom available."

Sabin swallowed. He hadn't thought about this eventuality yet, but it looked like he was going to have to, and soon. "That will be perfect. Thank you for hosting us," he said.

"I wish I had something better for you, but as you can see, our town is small."

"It's nothing you have to worry about. After spending a few nights on the road, I'm sure that whatever you have ready for us will be perfect."

Ysmal grinned. "I suspect you're right. Personally, I don't spend time in the desert if I can avoid it."

Sabin wished he could say the same, but unfortunately, he couldn't avoid the desert. At least this time around, it was a much nicer trip.

He'd been walking as much as possible so he could be next to Zeno as they traveled. He'd caught the guards staring at them a few times, but he didn't care what they thought. It wasn't like he and Zeno could do anything that the guards wouldn't hear, anyway. They had to know there was nothing between them.

"I'll show you to your room," Ysmal said.

He gestured at Sabin to follow him. Sabin fell into step with him. They walked into the house, and Sabin looked around, curious.

It wasn't huge by any means and nothing like the palace, but it was homey. A female demon stood by the entrance, and she bowed at Sabin when he entered her home. Sabin was used to people bowing at him, but it made him feel awkward in this situation. He was invading these people's home, and it didn't sit right with him. He could have offered to sleep in the cart, but he doubted Ysmal would have been okay with that. Just like Sabin needed to keep up appearances, so did he. It wouldn't look good if he let Berith's representative sleep in a cart.

"Now, I know this will be nothing like the palace, but it's the best I can offer you," he warned as he climbed the stairs to the upper level.

"Whatever you can give us will be perfect," Sabin tried to reassure him.

There were several closed doors down the hallway, and they walked past all of them until they reached the last one. Ysmal threw open the door, and Sabin found himself in front of a more than respectable bedroom. The bed occupied most of the space, and it seemed comfortable enough, certainly more comfortable than the cart in which Sabin had been sleeping. Someone had clearly changed the sheets recently, and probably that same someone had gathered a bunch of wildflowers and placed them in a vase by the window. Sabin couldn't help but wonder where they'd found the flowers. It wasn't like many of them grew in the desert.

"My wife made sure the room was clean and as comfortable as possible," Ysmal explained. "The room in front of yours is the bathroom. Feel free to use it anytime you need. I'm going to go downstairs and make sure your luggage is brought to you and that your guards have everything they need."

"Thank you."

"My wife is cooking dinner, but you have some time to relax and recuperate from your trip through the desert."

"I can use the rest, so once again, thank you." Sabin felt awkward, but then he didn't usually have to deal with this kind of people. At the palace, it was Berith's job to deal with vassals while Sabin stood in the background and took notes. He'd watched Berith enough to know more or less what he was supposed to do and what was expected of him, but still.

It wasn't his strong suit.

Ysmal left the room, closing the door behind him. Sabin eyed the bed. He was tempted to throw himself on it, but it would get the sheets dirty, and that would be a problem later tonight when he had to go to bed. Instead of doing that, he looked at Zeno. "What do you think? Are we safe?"

Zeno shrugged. "As safe as possible, considering the situation. I'll make sure nothing happens to you."

"Ysmal doesn't seem like the kind of demon who would attack me while I sleep."

"No one ever does."

Sabin swallowed. He supposed that Zeno wasn't wrong.

It wasn't the first time Zeno had visited this town, so he knew what to expect. The last time he'd been here, though, he hadn't been invited to sleep in the mayor's bed and to eat at his table.

He'd keep his hood down during the trip, even though it made him nervous. The hood was too recognizable, and he didn't want people freaking out when they realized The Mercenary was eating dinner in front of them. He couldn't afford to when he was supposed to watch Sabin and keep him safe.

He hadn't been sure what to expect from this trip, even though he knew why it was necessary. Now, as he listened to Sabin and Ysmal talk, he understood better. Sabin had a way of making people feel comfortable around him, and after only a few minutes at the table, Ysmal and his wife had relaxed. They'd started talking about life in their town and their children, who weren't anywhere to be seen. Apparently, the wife's sister was keeping an eye on them tonight. Zeno couldn't say he minded. He had no idea how to deal with children. Usually, he scared them, so it was better they stay as far away as possible from him.

"I doubt you want to talk about work tonight," Ysmal said.

"Oh, but that's why I'm here," Sabin told him with a smile. "Tell me whatever you need, and I'll listen."

Zeno wasn't surprised when the mayor launched himself into a list of things he needed help with. Sabin wasn't taking any notes since they were sitting at the dinner table, but he was clearly listening. He nodded and hummed along with the mayor's words, clearly making him feel like he was the most important thing in the room. It kind of made Zeno jealous, but he pushed away the feeling. Sabin was working, and so should he.

He was glad when dinner was finally over. It felt like Sabin and Ysmal had been talking for hours, and that was probably true, but if they were getting back on the road tomorrow, Sabin needed rest. Zeno cleared his throat to get Sabin's attention, and Sabin instantly turned toward him.

"I suppose we should head upstairs to bed," he said, getting to his hooves. "It was a pleasure talking to you, Ysmal. I'll write down everything you told me tonight, and I'll make sure the prince gets a copy of it."

"Thank you," Ysmal said as he followed Sabin's lead and got up. "We don't want to be a bother, but life in the desert is harsh. We need all the help we can get to ensure the town isn't taken over by outlaws."

"I understand. I haven't always lived in the palace, and even if I had, my recent trips across the desert have shown me how important it is to protect our people. Berith will make sure nothing happens to this town. It'll take a while for me to get back to the palace, of course, but I'll make sure he gets my report."

Ysmal walked them upstairs after they said good night to his wife. He kept asking if Sabin needed anything else, and Sabin kept telling him that he was perfectly fine. Zeno almost slammed the door in the man's face, but he gave him a tight smile and closed it instead.

When he turned, Sabin had flopped on the bed. He looked

exhausted, and without thinking about it, Zeno moved toward him and sat next to him on the bed. He took one of Sabin's legs and raised it to his thighs, then massaged the muscles. Sabin made a surprised sound, but after a moment, he relaxed.

"That feels good," he said with a groan.

"You've been walking way more than you're used to. Your muscles are bound to be tight."

"Maybe I should spend more time in the cart tomorrow."

"You should have spent more time in the cart from the beginning. I don't understand why you haven't."

Sabin propped himself up on his elbows. "I wanted to walk with you."

Zeno shook his head. "If you want to talk, we can do so while you're in the cart."

"I know. I just wish we weren't traveling together because of work, you know?"

Zeno did know. Sometimes, when the guards were silent, it was easy to imagine that he and Sabin were alone in the desert like they'd been after he'd rescued Sabin. The conditions had been harsh, but Zeno had been happy to get to know Sabin and listen to him talk. They hadn't needed to be careful about what they said and how they behaved. They'd been free, and Zeno wanted that feeling back.

Zeno let go of Sabin's leg and turned to face him. Sabin leaned even closer, and if Zeno wasn't mistaken, he was staring at Zeno's lips.

"This trip isn't as bad as I expected it would be," Zeno admitted.

"It isn't as bad as I expected, either. The fact that you're here helps a lot."

Zeno licked his lips. Were they about to kiss? There was nothing he wanted more, but he was also terrified things would change between him and Sabin if they did. As it was, Sabin was Zeno's only friend. They'd be stuck together on this trip for a while longer, and things would be awkward, to say the least, if they tried something and it didn't work.

But Zeno hadn't become The Mercenary because he didn't take chances. It looked like Sabin wanted to kiss him, and he definitely wanted to kiss Sabin.

So he moved closer. He could almost feel Sabin's breath on his lips, and he smiled. It would have scared anyone else — *he* would have scared anyone else — but not Sabin.

Someone knocked on the door.

Sabin groaned and flopped back onto the bed. Zeno stared at him for a moment, then went to open after taking a moment to gather himself. Outside, he found Ysmal holding a tray. "I thought you'd want some snacks for the night," he said.

Zeno took it with a sigh. No matter how much he wanted to strangle the mayor, he wouldn't.

Chapter Fifteen

They were on the road again. Sabin was exhausted, and he couldn't wait to get back to the palace, but he couldn't deny he was having fun. Traveling with Zeno was so very different from how he'd been traveling before. For one, he and Zeno talked. Well, *he* talked. Zeno mostly listened to him, asked a few questions, and that was that. Sabin didn't mind, though. He knew he could be a lot, and his friends regularly teased him about talking too much, but Zeno hadn't said anything about that. He just walked beside the cart, nodding and smiling as Sabin poured out his life story.

By now, Sabin had told him everything about his family. He'd told him how he, Berith, and Lon had met and how they'd become friends. He'd told him how Berith had become a prince of Hell and how he'd asked him and Lon to stay by his side because there was no one he trusted more. Now, he'd moved on to telling Zeno about Mel and how he and Berith had met.

But today, Zeno wasn't listening.

Sabin kept an eye on him as he continued talking. "So this demon thought that Berith would kill Mel or something like that. Berith would never do something so horrible, but he wanted to send Mel back to the human realm. Of course, he couldn't, because Mel had been a gift, and it would have looked bad."

Zeno nodded, but Sabin was pretty sure he hadn't heard a word of what he'd just said.

"So instead, he declared that Mel was the new prince of

Hell and that he'd be his slave forever and carry his babies. Everyone agreed, and here we are."

Zeno nodded again, and Sabin sighed. He'd known Zeno wasn't listening, and he didn't have a problem with that. He just wished he could help Zeno with whatever he was thinking about. Maybe he could. It wouldn't hurt to ask, at the very least.

He gently elbowed Zeno, making him jerk back. That was odd, because Zeno would have seen him move in any other circumstance, and he wouldn't have reacted that way. Sabin wasn't scared of being in danger because Zeno was distracted. He didn't care about that, especially with thirty guards walking around them.

"What's going on in that mind of yours?" he asked.

Zeno smiled, but it was clearly forced. "Nothing. I was listening to you."

"That's why you didn't say anything when I told you that Mel was the new prince of Hell?"

Zeno blinked. "You did?"

"I knew you weren't listening to me, and I wanted to test it. I was right."

"I'm sorry. I'll listen from now on."

Sabin shook his head and grabbed Zeno's arm. "That's not what I'm worried about. I know I talk a lot, and I don't expect you to listen to every word I say. If I'm bothering you, though, please let me know."

"You're not bothering me."

"Well, something clearly is."

Zeno looked around as if he were afraid someone was listening to them. He wasn't wrong. With all the guards around them, there was no way for them to have any privacy while they were on the road.

"It's just something about the next town we're visiting," Zeno said. His voice was soft enough that the guards wouldn't hear him as long as they stayed where they were.

Sabin moved even closer until their sides brushed against each other. "What is it? You don't have to tell me if you don't feel up for it, but I'd like to know."

"It's the town where I grew up."

That wasn't what Sabin had expected. For some reason, he hadn't thought about Zeno's life as a child, but Zeno *had* been a child. He hadn't been born the demon he was now, so it made sense that he had a hometown. "Your hometown."

Zeno nodded. "Exactly."

"Do you still have family here?" Sabin was careful because he didn't know anything about Zeno's past. He had no way to know if Zeno had a family or if anything had happened to them. The last thing he wanted was to push too hard and send Zeno running. He'd always been closed-lipped about himself, and Sabin suspected that being in this town wouldn't change that, not the right way anyway.

Zeno sighed and looked around again. "I never had any family, at least not anyone who was blood-related."

So he'd grown up without parents, or at least, without parents he'd known. It sounded like he had someone, though, and Sabin was curious. Still, he kept his mouth shut and focused on the road under his hooves. If Zeno wanted to tell him what happened to him as a child, he would. It would be no use pushing him.

Still, Sabin's heart broke for Zeno. It was clear from his voice that whatever had happened hurt him, even though years had passed. Maybe he thought his parents had abandoned him, and maybe he was right. Maybe his parents had died, and maybe they wanted him. He'd never know, unfortunately. He'd always have to ask himself where he came from, and while it wasn't something Sabin could ever fully understand, he knew something about it because of Lon.

Sabin wanted to reach for Zeno, maybe hug him, but he felt that Zeno would close off if he did. It couldn't be easy for him to tell Sabin any of this, and Sabin wanted to give him the space he needed to do so if he felt up for it.

"Let's just say that life here wasn't easy," Zeno said gruffly.

Sabin swallowed. He wasn't surprised something bad had happened in Berith's territory, and besides, from the sound of it, it had happened before Berith became prince. Still, it hurt to hear that Zeno the child had needed to fight to survive and grow up like countless other children. He made a mental note to ask Berith about that once he was back at the palace. If it was still happening, he wanted it to stop.

"But I survived, and I wasn't the only one. I left this town. I mostly stayed in the desert, especially in the beginning."

He was skipping a lot, but that was okay. "And that's how you became The Mercenary?"

"Eventually, yes."

"I'm sorry for whatever happened to you." Sabin hesitated. "We could skip this town?"

"What do you mean?"

"Well, it doesn't hold good memories for you. We don't have to go through this town if you feel like you shouldn't. We could just skip it and move on to our next stop."

Zeno hesitated, and Sabin thought he'd say yes for a moment. He wasn't surprised when Zeno shook his head, though.

"No. I might not have been back since I left, but I can do this."

"I never said anything about you not being able to do it. I just don't want you to have to think about the past when there is no need for you to."

"But there is. You have to talk to the mayor, don't you?"

Sabin did, and it would be better if they stopped here. Still, he was ready to do pretty much anything for Zeno and to keep him happy. "I could have him write to the palace."

"But then he'd wonder why you didn't stop here while you stopped everywhere else."

That much was true. "Then I could go on my own. You

might be my bodyguard, but nothing says that you have to come with me. You could walk around the town and wait for us on the other side."

Sabin already knew Zeno's answer to that, so he wasn't surprised when Zeno shook his head again. "I'm not abandoning you," Zeno said.

"I wouldn't think you were abandoning me."

"I'm coming with you, Sabin. You can stop trying to convince me to let you go alone, because that's not going to happen."

Sabin hadn't expected it to, and it was clear he wouldn't be able to do anything to change Zeno's mind. He didn't want to be away from Zeno, but he also didn't want to hurt him. He had no idea what the right decision was, so he supposed he'd let Zeno take the lead once more.

Zeno wasn't a coward, and he wasn't afraid. He could face this town, and after he did, he'd come out on the other side in one piece. He wouldn't allow his past to guide his actions, just like he hadn't allowed it or anything and anyone else to do so since he'd left. He had no intention of letting Sabin do anything on his own, and not just because he was Sabin's bodyguard. Sabin meant a lot to him, and he wouldn't risk him.

He was relieved when Sabin nodded and gave him a tiny smile. "You can come with me, of course. I was just trying to make things easier on you," he murmured.

"I'm grateful for that, but you need to let *me* worry about this. I know you want to help, but I have to face this."

Zeno should have done so long ago, but he'd never thought he'd come back. He'd been nearby a few times, but he'd always avoided the town, even though he couldn't help but wonder if some of his foster siblings were still here. When he was in his area, his thoughts were never far from Tobal, his favorite brother. He'd left him behind, even though they'd promised each other they'd always been there for the other.

Zeno had broken that promise.

As soon as their master had died, he'd run. He hadn't waited for Tobal. He'd been terrified that their master's partner would continue to work them to death, and he'd needed out. He had no idea what happened to Tobal, but not a day passed that he didn't feel guilty about the way he'd dumped his brother.

And now he was here. He might be about to find out what had happened to his brother, and he wasn't sure he was ready for that. He wasn't sure he ever would be, but there was no avoiding this town. Sabin needed to talk to the mayor, and there was no way out of that. Besides, Zeno doubted anyone would recognize him. He was just another demon walking through town. There was nothing special about him, and even if the people he'd grown up with weren't all dead, what would be the odds that they'd recognize him?

"You could pull up your hood," Sabin offered.

Zeno had been distracted since that morning when he'd looked at the map and the itinerary and had realized where they were headed. He'd seen it before when they were still at the palace, but he'd managed to ignore it. He couldn't anymore, and he'd been too distracted to be efficient as Sabin's bodyguard. No matter how many times he berated himself to be more careful and stop obsessing, he hadn't managed.

"I don't want people to recognize me as The Mercenary," he explained.

"I don't think they will. I mean, you're not the only demon who walks around with their face covered. Even if they do recognize you, though, why would it be a problem?"

"I've never aligned myself with anyone as The Mercenary," Zeno explained. "If they recognize me and realize I'm your bodyguard, they'll think I work for the prince now."

"And isn't that the case? I don't know anything about your business, but if anyone realizes who you are and that you're working for Berith, they'll probably believe that he hired you for something, just like countless other people hired you in the past. I doubt it would do anything to your reputation."

Zeno agreed. Actually, his reputation might get better because he was working for a prince of Hell. He hesitated for a moment longer, but in the end, he grabbed his hood and pulled it up. When he turned to Sabin, it was to find him smiling. He didn't look smug, but rather relieved.

That made Zeno realize how much Sabin cared about him. He didn't understand what he'd done to deserve this kind of affection. Sabin could have so many other demons, including demons who lived at the palace and who were perfect for him. Instead, for some reason, he wanted Zeno.

Nothing made sense anymore.

He was relieved when nothing else happened. They continued walking toward the town, and Sabin continued talking about whatever passed through his mind. Zeno stayed silent, but Sabin had never expected him to answer most of his questions. He was happy just talking, and Zeno wanted him to be. Still, he grew more tense the closer they walked to town, and once they stood in front of it, he almost turned and ran. The only reason he didn't was that Sabin was beside him.

"It's small," Sabin said as he looked at the scattered houses in front of them.

Zeno had been holding his breath, but the big house by the town wall in which he and the others had lived was gone. There was no sign of it, and he didn't know what to think about that. When had it been destroyed? *Why* had it been destroyed? In this area of the desert, it would have been stupid to do something like that. Even if the master's partner had died or left, it would have been better to use the building for something else.

"All right?" Sabin asked.

Zeno nodded. He needed to focus on Sabin and keeping him safe, not on his past.

Sabin didn't ask him twice. Instead, he climbed into the cart so that he'd be sitting down when they faced the mayor, and they started moving again.

Nothing else had changed. The rest of the town was the same as it had been once, and that made Zeno nervous. He led the way toward the mayor's house, wondering what they'd find there.

Every town in the desert was similar. They all had an external wall to protect them from predators who came out at night. The wall was usually wooden for small towns, but sometimes it was stone. It was always stronger the larger the town was because there were more people to protect and more people who could work on it.

Here, the wall was made of wood, and the door was open. Two guards stared at them as they came closer, unmoving. Zeno expected them to stop Sabin, but instead, they waved at him and the guards to walk through. They either sucked at keeping the town safe or knew who Sabin was. That wouldn't be surprising. By now, word had gone around that Sabin was visiting Berith's vassals, and besides, the mayor and the other people in charge had been notified about his visit.

The town was so small that it was no trouble finding the mayor's house, even if Zeno hadn't already known where it was. It was right smack in the middle, and while it wasn't big, it was larger than the other houses around it. The only larger house had been the one where Zeno had grown up, and it was gone.

When they reached the mayor's house, he was waiting for them in front. Zeno was startled to see that it wasn't the same mayor who'd been in charge when he was a child. He didn't recognize this demon, but he hoped he was a better person than the old mayor, who'd known what was happening in that house and hadn't done anything to help. Zeno suspected that mayor had earned something from it, which was why he'd never stopped it.

"Welcome to our small town," the mayor said smoothly.

Zeno helped Sabin out of the cart. He kept his hood up, hiding from the world and everyone who might recognize him as Zeno.

Sabin gave Zeno a worried glance, but he was here to do a job, so he turned his attention to the mayor. "Thank you. My name is Sabin, and I'm prince Berith's representative."

"I'm Ornet, the mayor of this town. Come in, come in."

Sabin glanced at Zeno, and Zeno nodded. Sabin wasn't going anywhere without him, which meant they'd both go into the house.

Zeno swallowed. He didn't like how this town made him feel, but they wouldn't be here long. Tomorrow they'd be on the road again, and he'd never have to see this place again. That was what he focused on as he followed Sabin into the mayor's house.

Sabin could tell Zeno was distracted. He wouldn't have allowed the mayor to come so close to Sabin if he hadn't been. Ornet wasn't a bad-looking demon, but he was a bit pushy with his attention, and Sabin wished he wasn't. He had no interest in sleeping with the mayor or anyone who wasn't Zeno.

"I can't begin to tell you how happy I am to have you in my town," Ornet said as he pressed a hand to the small of Sabin's back and led him deeper into the house. "I have a room ready for you. It's right next to mine."

Sabin took a step to the side, relieved when Ornet's hand dropped. He didn't think the mayor was trying to be nasty about it, but he was definitely flirting.

"I'm surprised to see such a beautiful demon has been sent out on the road by himself," Ornet continued. "Although, of course, I understand why it was necessary. I've heard a lot about you and how you're the prince's right-hand man."

Sabin forced himself to smile. "I am, and I was the only

logical choice when it came to representing Berith. As for the bedroom, I'm sure it will be perfect for my bodyguard and me."

Ornet blinked. It was as if he hadn't even noticed that Zeno was there. Zeno had been completely silent, so maybe it wasn't a surprise. Still, Sabin wanted to be clear that nothing would be happening between him and Ornet. He didn't want to be rude about it or offend the mayor, so the best way to do it was to point out that they'd never be alone. Most demons wanted some privacy when they seduced someone.

Sabin hoped Ornet wasn't one of the demons who enjoyed public sex.

"You're safe in my house," Ornet promised.

"I'm sure I am, but the prince was clear. My bodyguard is to be with me at all times."

"Well, there's only one bed."

"It won't be a problem."

Sabin wasn't about to explain that he and Zeno had been sharing a bed since day one. Initially, it had been awkward, because neither of them had known how to behave. After waking up in Zeno's arms a few times, Sabin had gotten over it. He was pretty sure Zeno knew how he felt about him. The fact that he hadn't done anything was a clear sign that Zeno didn't feel the same, but that was okay. Sabin had never expected him to. He'd be fine as long as his feelings didn't make Zeno run.

"Of course. I apologize."

"There's nothing to apologize for, and I thank you for being so thoughtful."

"Well, I'm sure you'd like some time to wash up. I have invited several prominent people who live in town for dinner tonight, but since you're here, maybe you want to visit the flower fields?"

Sabin had made a point of learning what he could about the towns he'd be visiting, so he knew about the flower fields.

They were at the back of the town, hidden in a deep valley surrounded by mountains. They were an oddity in the desert, and he had to admit he'd been excited about seeing them. They grew there naturally, and as far as he knew, the town didn't do anything for their upkeep, which made them even more of a miracle.

"I'd love to visit the fields," he told Ornet. "My bodyguard and I will go after we wash up." This way, he'd make sure Ornet wouldn't be inviting himself to come along.

The mayor was clearly disappointed, but he didn't push. "Well, follow me. I'll show you to your room, and I'll let everyone know you've arrived. Dinner will be in a few hours. I hope that's all right."

"It's perfectly fine." That way, Sabin and Zeno would have a few hours to relax, although Sabin wasn't sure Zeno would be able to do so, considering where they were.

He'd been stunned to find out this was where Zeno had grown up, and knowing that meant he wasn't quite sure how to behave. He was acting as if this was just another town, but for Zeno, it wasn't.

Ornet showed them to the room like he'd promised, and Sabin was more than happy to lock himself inside. One of the guards would be by soon with the chest that contained his belongings, so he'd be able to change, but right now, he wanted to check on Zeno and make sure he was okay.

"How are you feeling?" he asked.

"I'm fine," Zeno said gruffly. "You should wash up. I'll wait for the chest."

"You're sure? We can still leave this town."

"We won't. This is where we should be, and you have work to do tonight."

"You know I'd happily sacrifice this dinner for your happiness, right?"

Zeno stared at Sabin for a moment before nodding. "I know. But you won't have to. I can deal with this, and I will."

Sabin had no doubt that he would, but he wished Zeno didn't have to. He wanted to help him, but he didn't know if there was a way for him to do so.

So instead, he did what Zeno had said and went to the bathroom to wash up. The mayors they'd visited reserved their best bedroom for him, and usually, there was a private bathroom. He was glad this room had one, mostly so he wouldn't have to cross paths with Ornet in the hallway. He wasn't sure Zeno had noticed what Ornet had been doing. If he had, he hadn't said anything about it.

Sabin was relieved to be able to wash up with some water. It was far from the bath he would normally take if he were at the palace, but it was better than keeping the dust and sand all over him. By the time he was done, he felt like a new demon, and he was glad to see that Zeno had relaxed when he went back to the bedroom.

Zeno took his own turn in the bathroom while Sabin dressed, and once they were both done, Zeno gestured at the door. "We can go see the fields now."

"I assume you know the way?"

"I do."

Sabin followed Zeno out the door. The mayor was in the entrance, talking to someone, but he smiled at Sabin when he heard him and Zeno. "Going to the fields?"

"We are. We'll be back in a few hours."

"Dinner should be ready by then. We'll be waiting for you."

"Thank you." Sabin was glad to be able to leave the house. He didn't think Ornet was a bad person, but he made him uneasy.

Most of the guards had disappeared, no doubt to wash up and get some food. The head guard was still by one of the carts, and Sabin nodded at her as he walked past.

Being without the guards felt freeing, especially once they left town through the back and no one was staring at him anymore. Sabin relaxed, and he even found himself smiling again.

"I used to spend a lot of time in these fields as a child," Zeno suddenly said.

"Did you?"

"They were an escape from everything that was happening in my life. My brother and I went there almost every day."

It was the first time Zeno mentioned a brother, and Sabin held his breath.

"You don't have to tell me about any of this," he said when Zeno didn't continue.

"I know, but maybe I want to."

Sabin didn't insist. He let Zeno guide him down a small road, looking around for the flowers. They took a sharp turn around a tall wall of stone, and Sabin sucked in a breath at the sight that waited for them on the other side.

As far as he could see, surrounded by stone, were flowers. Most of them were purple, although they looked more dark pink in a few spots. It was a small piece of heaven in a hellish place, and he couldn't believe he was so lucky to be able to see it.

He was startled when Zeno took his hand. Zeno smiled at him and pulled, headed toward the nearest field.

"Come on. Let's sit down," he said.

Sabin could only nod and follow his lead.

Zeno couldn't believe he was back. He wasn't sure how to feel about it, but Sabin's presence by his side made it easier to ignore the memories of the past and focus on the present. Zeno couldn't ignore Sabin even if he wanted to, and right now, he didn't. Sabin was the center of Zeno's universe, no matter how strange and odd it was for Zeno to feel that way.

He wasn't sure what to do or say, or even if he should do or say something. It was peaceful to sit here, surrounded by flowers that matched Sabin's hair and the fur on his legs. Sabin was more beautiful than any flower could ever be, though. Zeno wanted to tell him that, but the words stuck on his tongue every time he tried. He wasn't one for romance, and he had no idea where to start when it came to that.

But Sabin deserved romance, so Zeno cleared his throat and tried. "You're, err, beautiful."

Sabin arched an elegant brow. "Am I?"

How was Zeno supposed to answer what? "Yes. Your hair matches the flowers." He was pretty sure he was doing an awful job, so maybe it would be better for him to keep his mouth shut from now on.

He pressed his lips together and looked away. There was a reason he tended to stay on his own and didn't have relationships, dammit. He sucked at this, and he was pretty sure that if Sabin could hear his stream of thought, he'd run away screaming.

"Thank you. This place is beautiful, much more than I am," Sabin said softly.

Zeno frowned. "I think you're prettier."

"And I think you're biased."

"If I were, it would be in favor of the flowers."

"True. You really spent your childhood here?"

Zeno usually did his best not to think of his childhood. Almost all of it had been shit except for the moments he'd spent here with Tobal. For some reason, thinking of Tobal hurt almost as much as the bad memories. Zeno hadn't seen him since he'd left this place with the intention of never coming back. He'd clearly been wrong about that — although they wouldn't be here if it weren't for Sabin — and he couldn't help but wonder if Tobal was still around. Had he decided to stay here, where they grew up, or had he left, too? Zeno wanted to see him, yet, at the same time, he didn't. Would seeing Tobal remind Zeno of their harsh childhood? Probably, but then everything here did already.

"I did," Zeno confirmed. He'd never told anyone about this place, but he found himself telling Sabin. "I never knew my parents. Someone found me as a child and took me in. I was lucky, I guess, even though life was rough."

"So it wasn't a family who took you in?"

"No. Even though I was about six years old, I was put to work. We all were."

Sabin's body tensed next to Zeno. "I know this is how things work in Hell, but sometimes, I wonder if humans aren't better than us."

"I doubt all humans are angels." Zeno wouldn't be surprised if some of them did things that even demons wouldn't contemplate.

"I suppose not. But you were a child. You deserved someone who took care of you, at the very least. Instead, you were put to work. I can only imagine what you went through, but I imagine it's a miracle you're still alive."

It was. Many of the demons Zeno had grown up with had died in their childhood. He and Tobal were among the few who hadn't.

Sabin made a sound that was too close to a sob. Zeno turned to him, horrified to have made Sabin cry, but Sabin threw himself at him before he could say anything. Zeno hadn't expected it, and while he managed to catch Sabin, they tilted backward. Zeno wrapped his arms tightly around Sabin and took the brunt of the hit as they landed in the middle of the flowers.

They were surrounded by a purple, fragrant pillow. The sky above them was red, turning to black, but the only thing Zeno could see was Sabin.

His eyes were wide and full of tears. As Zeno stared, one escaped and rolled down Sabin's cheek, and Zeno moved before he could think better of it. He pushed forward and caught the tear with his lips, freezing when he realized what he'd done.

What was he thinking? There was no way Sabin wanted this with him.

But when Zeno flopped back down, already thinking about rolling Sabin off him and running away, Sabin kissed him. Zeno opened his mouth in a croak, and Sabin swept in, pushing his tongue inside and making Zeno his with only one touch.

Or maybe Zeno was already his. Maybe this was just Sabin marking Zeno for everyone to see, including Zeno.

Zeno had been resisting this for a long time, but now he stopped. He held Sabin against him with one hand and buried the other in Sabin's hair. It was soft and silky on Zeno's rough skin, but Sabin didn't seem to care. He kissed Zeno as if it was the only time they'd do this, as if he wanted to make the most out of it.

So did Zeno. At this moment, Sabin was everything, Zeno's entire world, and Zeno never wanted it to end.

He felt Sabin harden against him. His own cock slid out of its pouch, ready to play, but both Zeno and Sabin were too frantic even to push their clothing away. The short tunic Sabin wore exposed his legs, and Zeno ran a hand up and down Sabin's furry thigh, smiling at the little groans that escaped from Sabin's throat. He took a risk, sliding his hand up and under Sabin's tunic, cupping one ass cheek.

Sabin pressed harder against Zeno and bit Zeno's lip. Zeno tasted blood, but he didn't care. Sabin could bite him any time he wanted, as hard as he wanted.

They rutted against each other. It was too much and not enough at the same time, and Zeno chased the pleasure Sabin could give him. Sabin groaned and thrust and did the same until he stiffened against Zeno. Zeno felt warm wetness spread on his pants, just over his pouch, and his cock jerked. Sabin had come on him. He'd marked him with his scent and his essence, and while Zeno wanted Sabin *inside* of him, this was good, too, so good that he came, too.

Sabin didn't stop moving until Zeno slumped under him. They stayed there, surrounded by purple flowers and a red sky until Sabin chuckled.

"I can't say I expected this."

"I didn't, either. But I don't regret it." If anything, Zeno was wondering when they'd do it again. He couldn't get enough of Sabin.

"Me, neither." Sabin sat up, kissed Zeno, then got to his feet. "But the guards will come to find us if we don't head back soon."

Unfortunately, he was right, and since Zeno didn't want anyone else to see Sabin in this state, he followed Sabin's lead. It took a moment to straighten their clothes to at least appear like they hadn't been up to anything, and while they couldn't do much about the stickiness in their clothes, at least most demons wouldn't realize what they'd been up to.

Sabin took Zeno's hand and pulled him toward the road. Zeno followed, only to tense when he noticed someone leaning against the fence. Had they been spying? Zeno couldn't see much of the demon from a distance, just that their skin was pale and marked and that they had a tail.

Something snapped under Zeno's foot, and the demon jumped and turned. Zeno sucked in a breath, unable to speak. Now he could see the demon had red marks all over his skin, red hands, and yellow eyes—all three of them. The third was placed above the first two, in the middle of his forehead. The demon's dark curly hair hid the tiny horns Zeno knew were there.

"Well, that's not what we used to do in that field," the demon drawled.

Sabin looked from the demon to Zeno, clearly confused.

"I never wanted to do anything like that with you, Tobal," Zeno answered.

Tobal laughed. "Thank fuck, because that would have been awkward." He hesitated. "When I heard you were in town, I knew I'd find you here. I just didn't expect to find you in this kind of . . . position." He looked Sabin up and down. "Or with such a beautiful demon."

Zeno huffed. It looked like his brother hadn't changed one bit. "Sabin, this is Tobal, my foster brother. Tobal, this is Sabin." Zeno's everything.

Chapter Sixteen

Sabin couldn't help but peek at Zeno and his brother as they walked in front of his cart. The two were mostly silent, but they seemed close. Maybe it was something they shared.

He couldn't believe Zeno had opened up to him so much or anything else that had happened in the field. He wanted him and Zeno to talk about it, but it felt impossible with Tobal following them on the road. Sabin wanted to know what Zeno expected from him and what was happening between them, but he didn't dare bring it up.

Zeno already had enough to deal with. He'd been stunned when he'd seen his brother, but from Sabin's point of view, it was as if they'd never lost sight of each other. As soon as they saw each other again, they started teasing and talking, and Sabin hadn't believed his eyes. Zeno was like another person with his brother, and Sabin was a bit jealous, even though he could see that Zeno was different with him, too. Zeno clearly trusted him as much as he trusted Tobal, but they didn't share the same story.

Sabin had been glad to leave Zeno's hometown behind a few days ago and stunned when they'd found Tobal waiting for them at the entrance of town. He'd been carrying a bag, and when he'd seen them, he declared he was coming with them. He and Zeno hadn't had many opportunities to talk to each other while they'd been in town, so it made sense.

After they'd left the field, Tobal had walked them back to the mayor's house. He and Zeno had been silent, but they kept bumping their shoulders against each other, and it felt like a silent communication between two siblings. Sabin did the same with some of his siblings, so he understood.

Once they'd reached the mayor's house, they'd found it full of people. The mayor had said he'd invited a few people, but it was much more than that. Zeno had gone into protective mode, and Tobal had left with the promise they'd talk soon.

And they had. Tobal had surprised them the next morning, but Zeno had taken it in stride. He'd been clearly confused for a moment, then when Tobal had explained he was coming with them, a flash of happiness had crossed his face. He'd pulled down his hood when Tobal had asked him why he wore it, and he hadn't pulled it back up again. Sabin supposed that now they were far from his hometown, he felt more secure with people seeing his face.

He wasn't about to protest. He liked seeing Zeno's face and his expressions.

Sabin was glad he knew more about Zeno's back story now. It made it easier to understand why Zeno was the way he was, and that was all Sabin had wanted. Well, *almost* all he'd wanted. He still needed to find out what was happening between them, but it could wait.

He was surprised when, after they stopped for lunch, Zeno moved from his brother's side to being close to Sabin. Sabin was walking again, even though it was hot, so maybe it was because of that.

"You didn't walk this morning," Zeno said.

Sabin smiled at him. "I wanted to give you and your brother time to be together."

"We could have done that with you next to us."

"Maybe, but I felt that you needed time on your own."

Zeno stared at him for a moment. Sabin almost stumbled on his own hoof under the intensity of Zeno's gaze. He swallowed, wondering what Zeno was about to say. Whatever it was, it seemed serious.

"About what happened in the field," Zeno started.

Sabin raised a hand. "We don't have to talk about it. I understand that your focus is on your brother right now, and that's all right."

"It's not. You don't deserve for me to ignore you, especially after what happened."

"You haven't been ignoring me. I'm just saying that there's time for us to talk about this and that I'm fine waiting."

Sabin really wasn't. He wanted to know what was happening between him and Zeno, but he was terrified that Zeno was about to tell him it had been a one-time thing. Sabin wanted so much more, and he thought Zeno did, too, but how could he be sure?

Zeno nodded once. "You're right that we have time to talk about it. I just wanted you to know that you matter to me, Sabin. What we did mattered."

Sabin's chest felt tight. "It did?"

"I never want you to think otherwise. I don't know what will happen between us or in general, but I care about you."

Sabin couldn't help the smile that spread his lips. "I care about you, too."

Zeno stared for a moment, then he nodded. "All right. The next place on our list will be different."

Sabin blinked at the change of topic, but he went with it. Zeno wasn't one to talk about his emotions, so what had just happened between them had probably pushed him to his limit. Now, he was ready to focus on their job, and that was fine with Sabin. "It will. So far, we've visited mostly small towns. The next place will be a city, and the person who will welcome us won't be a mayor, but rather, an earl."

"Which is lower than the prince but higher than a mayor."

"Definitely. We have several earls in our territory and a few dukes, which is even higher."

"All of this was easier when I didn't care about who was who," Zeno grumbled.

Sabin almost laughed. "I agree it would be easier without

these titles, but you know demons. They care about them, and really, it's to our advantage. We just have to remember that technically, I'm a prince."

"Because you're Berith's representative."

"Exactly. Everyone has to treat me as if I were him, because normally he'd be the one making this trip."

"What do I have to look for once we reach the city?"

"Have you ever been here?"

"A few times, but usually I keep to the worst part of the city, and I hide as much as possible."

Because otherwise, people would start to panic if they found out that The Mercenary was in town. Although Sabin disliked how isolated Zeno had been until they'd met, it made sense. It partly was because Zeno had wanted it, but still.

They talked about the city and what to expect from the earl for a while longer, until Sabin could see the city in the distance and had to climb into the cart. If he was honest, he was eager to get there. It would be the first time since he'd left the palace that he'd be able to take a bath, and he couldn't wait. The rooms where he and Zeno had been placed during their visits to the small towns had been nice, but nothing like what Sabin was used to. He didn't even care about the bed. He just wanted a bath.

It took them a few days to reach the palace. Sabin wished they could go faster, but between the carts and the nuckelavee, it wasn't possible. This was the last stop before they headed home, though, and he couldn't wait. At the same time, he also didn't want to get home, because it might mean the end of what was growing between him and Zeno.

There was no way for him or anyone to visit the entirety of Berith's territory, but thankfully, he wouldn't have to. Most of the affluent demons who lived there, the earls and the dukes and the barons, visited Berith's palace as often as they could. It gave them clout to be seen with the prince.

But he'd deal with that when he couldn't avoid it anymore.

Their arrival in the city was very different from the small towns they'd visited. As soon as one of the guards noticed them from the high city walls, they sent word to the earl that they'd arrived. By the time they reached the gate, the earl had sent someone to welcome them. They were ushered into the city and toward the palace, with dozens of guards belonging to the earl keeping the crowd away. Sabin wasn't used to this. Even at home in the city, he was allowed to leave the palace on his own. Did the earl expect him to be attacked? Or was he just trying to show Sabin respect?

Sabin relaxed once they reached the palace. He knew how to behave here in a way he didn't know in the desert. He hadn't been born in the palace, but he'd been there for several years now, and it was his home. As far as he was concerned, it was easier to deal with the people who were already trying to get his attention than with small-town mayors.

"Welcome," a tall demon said as she came down the stairs in front of which they'd stopped. "My name is Liora. The earl will see you soon, but he thought you'd want to wash up and eat something before he did."

Sabin smiled at her. She'd just given him the best news of the day. "I would love to be able to take a bath."

She smiled, exposing her fangs. "Your rooms are ready for you."

"My bodyguard will be staying with me."

She didn't even blink at that. She was probably used to it, just like Sabin. It made sense for visiting dignitaries to want to keep their bodyguards close. "Of course. If you'll follow me, I'll show you the way. The servants will take care of your luggage and, of course, will refill your cart with food and water."

Sabin could have kissed her. Instead, he climbed out of the cart in which he'd sat again once they reached the city and followed her, Zeno right behind him. They both looked back at Tobal one last time, but he waved at them to go ahead. He'd be staying with the guards, and he'd seemed happy about that when Sabin had told him. In general, Tobal seemed to be happy about many things, but Sabin couldn't tell if it was just how he was or because he'd found Zeno again.

He supposed he'd find out in time.

They were back in a palace, and Zeno was uncomfortable. He was also torn between wanting to go back to Tobal and sticking by Sabin's side. But he and Tobal had talked, and Tobal had insisted Zeno needed to stay with Sabin. They'd have all the time they needed to talk and fix their relationship once they left the city. For now, Zeno needed to keep Sabin safe, and that meant he had to get his head in the game.

He and Sabin followed the demon who'd welcomed them through the palace. She pointed out several rooms, which made Zeno wonder why. It wasn't like he and Sabin were going to stick around long enough to use all of them. But at least he'd know where everything was, and it might come in useful, so he didn't say anything about it.

He'd spent enough time in Berith's palace to recognize when the hallways changed. The decoration was different in the most private part of the palace, so he wasn't surprised when Liora paused in front of a door and gestured at it. "This will be your room for the length of your stay with us," she said. "I'll have servants bring you food and your personal belongings. The bath should already be drawn, but if you need anything else, feel free to ask one of the servants to look for me."

Sabin smiled easily. "I'm sure everything will be perfect. Thank you."

She gave them a little bow, then quickly walked down the hallway. Sabin pushed open the door, and Zeno followed him in.

He wasn't surprised about anything in the room. This had

to be a guest bedroom like the one he'd been staying in at Berith's palace, but it was more luxurious than anything Zeno had seen in his life, even that bedroom. Berith might be a prince, but he was more understated than this earl.

The space was divided into rooms. The first room, which they'd stepped into from the hallway, contained a sitting area. The wide doors were open and let in a breeze, and from the windows, Zeno could see a garden similar to the one Berith had in his palace. There was food on a small table, as well as drinks. There was a lot of wood and gold, and Zeno resisted the urge to squint.

He stepped deeper into the room and looked around. The second room held the biggest bed he'd ever seen, and that included the bed he'd slept in while at Berith's palace. It was good it was so big, because it was the only bed there. He and Sabin would have plenty of space, although maybe, they wouldn't want it.

Zeno wasn't sure how things had changed between them, but they had. If it weren't for his brother, they'd probably have talked about what had happened in the flower field. Zeno wanted to know what it meant to both of them, but for now, it was enough for him to know that Sabin cared about him. They could talk about their relationship and whatever it meant once they were back at Berith's palace.

Sabin had already stepped through the open doorway to the bedroom and disappeared. Zeno quickly followed him, smiling when he found Sabin in the bathroom, taking off his clothes. He was standing in front of the massive bath—it was more like a small pool— and he looked excited.

He turned to look at Zeno, then realized he was mostly naked in front of him. His cheeks flushed, but he didn't hesitate to ditch the last article of clothing on his body and step into the bath.

"Come on in," he said.

Zeno blinked. "In the bath?"

"It's more than big enough for us."

"I should be guarding you, not taking a bath with you."

But Sabin was beautiful, all wet and waiting for him. Zeno could feel his resolve weakening, so he wasn't surprised when he couldn't resist when Sabin held out his hand.

He huffed and made sure Sabin knew he wasn't entirely happy about this, but in reality, he was glad to have this time alone with Sabin. Zeno was happy to have his brother back, but he wanted to focus on Sabin now.

He couldn't deny it felt good when he slid into the water. It was warm, almost too much, and he felt his muscles relax instantly. He moved further in, then submerged himself entirely. When he surfaced, it was to find Sabin leaning against the side of the bath, smiling softly.

"What?" Zeno asked as he pushed his hair away from his face.

"Nothing. You just look happy."

"I am."

"Because of Tobal."

"And because of you." Zeno swam closer to Sabin, stopping in front of him. "I like what we're doing." And Zeno didn't want it to stop.

Once Sabin was back at Berith's palace, it would be time for Zeno to leave. His work would be over, and he wouldn't have a reason to stay. Sabin would be reason enough, but Zeno wasn't sure he could live at the palace. Being there for only a few nights had made his skin crawl.

It wasn't anyone's fault. Everyone had been nice to him, even the servants. He just disliked living with so many people around him. He felt crowded, which was why he usually lived on his own in the middle of nowhere. He'd never get used to sharing living spaces with so many people, no matter how much he might want to.

And he did want to. He wanted to do everything for Sabin, but he had to accept his limitations. No matter how much he wanted to stay with Sabin, he wasn't sure either of them would be happy if he did. He was terrified that he'd come to resent Sabin, and that wasn't something he wanted to deal with. Sabin didn't deserve to be resented. He didn't deserve anything but to be loved, and Zeno had no idea if he could do that.

"You need to relax," Sabin said. He wrapped his arms around Zeno's neck and pulled him in for a kiss. Zeno was more than happy to go along with it and kiss him back. "I know you're nervous about having so many demons around you. I doubt any of them will attack us, though, and even if they try, I believe in you. You'll stop them, and no one will be able to hurt me."

"I'll make sure they don't."

"I know. I'm glad to have you with me during this trip, and I can't imagine anyone else doing the job you're doing. But right now, we're alone. There's no one with us, which means we won't be attacked."

Zeno looked around. "What about the servants?"

"They'll know better than to come into the bathroom when it's occupied. Come on, Zeno. Relax. Do it for me?"

Zeno doubted he'd ever be able to fully relax, no matter what Sabin was asking. But maybe, he could let go of some of his anxiousness and focus on who was in his arms.

Sabin.

He deserved to have Zeno's full attention, and Zeno intended to give it to him, even if it was only for an hour or so. Sabin was right. No one would try attacking them in the bath, which meant Zeno could make Sabin happy.

And he did.

CHAPTER SEVENTEEN

Sabin smiled at the earl, but he was barely listening to the demon. He couldn't stop thinking about Zeno, and he wasn't sure how to stop. He'd known that going on the road with Zeno would spell trouble for him, and he was right.

He'd fallen in love with Zeno. He'd tried not to, but it had been inevitable. He'd known it since day one, and he wasn't sure what to do now. He and Zeno needed to talk, but he felt that they shouldn't do so on the road. They were stuck together here, and if Zeno wanted to let Sabin down, it wouldn't be easy for him to do so.

"I'm sorry you're leaving so soon," the earl said with a smile.

He leaned closer to Sabin, and Sabin took a tiny step back. What was it with these people not understanding personal space? At least the mayor in Zeno's hometown hadn't been so pushy. The earl was, and he kept staring at Sabin as if he might eat him. Sabin wasn't even sure if it was in a pleasurable way or not. He'd heard things about this demon, and he wasn't about to ask if they were true. He was too afraid to.

"Unfortunately, duty calls me back to the palace," he said.

"You do a lot of work for the prince?"

"Well, I'm his personal assistant. I handle most of the day-to-day work."

"It would have been nice to see the prince, but seeing you was nicer."

The earl touched Sabin's forearm. He danced his fingers up to Sabin's shoulder, but when Sabin tried to move away, his back found the wall. He was trapped, and he didn't like that.

He looked around, trying to find Zeno. He'd never been far from Sabin during this trip, but this evening was different. The earl had organized a party, and no matter how many times Sabin had told him he was tired and wanted to rest, the earl hadn't taken no for an answer. Sabin wasn't surprised, considering how he was touching Sabin now, but he needed a way out. He knew Zeno was around here, but even though he was Sabin's bodyguard, or maybe because of that, he'd stayed out of sight.

Sabin needed to let the earl down without getting him angry at him. He wasn't sure that was possible, but the only alternative was to give the earl what he wanted, and Sabin wasn't about to do that.

"What are you doing?" someone asked with a growl.

Sabin almost kissed Zeno. He was standing behind the earl, looking like he might beat him into the floor.

The earl didn't seem to realize how dangerous Zeno was, and he barely gave him a glance. "Now, I know you said that you need to get back on the road tomorrow, but maybe I can convince you to stay for at least a few more days?" he asked Sabin. He pressed his palm to Sabin's arm and stroked up and down.

Sabin forced a smile on his lips and stepped sideways, trying to walk around the earl. "As I said, the prince expects me to come home as soon as possible."

"You could tell him you need a bit more rest before getting back on the road."

"I apologize, but that won't be possible."

"Have you ever thought about leaving Berith?"

Sabin had no idea where that came from. "No. He's not only my prince. He's also a dear friend, and I'm not planning on ever leaving his side. Now, if you'll excuse me, my bodyguard needs to inform me about the state of our convoy."

Sabin quickly sidestepped the earl, then grabbed Zeno's

arm and pulled him away. Zeno was more than happy to come along, and his expression was enough for the people in front of them to move away and let them pass.

Sabin had never enjoyed the fact that Zeno was so grumpy more than he did now.

"What was he doing to you?" Zeno asked loud enough that a few people turned to look at them.

Sabin leaned closer. He'd brought nice clothes so he wouldn't be out of place at the palace, but Zeno hadn't bothered. His tunic and pants were clean, but they were obviously made for travel in the desert, not for a party. Not that Zeno cared. He couldn't care less what the people around them thought of him. From his point of view, they weren't worth the energy it would take for him to worry over it.

"He was getting handsy, but he didn't do anything unforgivable."

"I can go back and kick his ass."

Sabin fought the urge to smile. "I'm sure you can, but it would be better if you didn't."

"Why not? Because he's an earl?"

"Exactly. He could easily have you imprisoned, and if he ever found out who you are, he'd put you to death or use you." And Sabin wasn't sure which one would be worse.

Zeno was still tense by his side, so he pulled him out of the room and into the garden. It had been decorated as much as the room in which the party was held, but there were fewer people here. The earl had gone all-in with costly flowers and expensive food, and while Sabin didn't blame him, he wished he'd been able to have a quiet evening with Zeno—and possibly with Tobal.

He wanted to get to know Zeno's brother, and he felt they'd barely talked.

Once they were outside, he took a deep breath. He felt Zeno relax, and he smiled when Zeno unhooked his arm from Sabin's and instead wrapped it around Sabin's waist. Sabin leaned against his side, happy to take a moment.

"You don't like this any more than I do," Zeno said.

"I really don't. But I understand why the earl felt he needed to organize a party. It's not every day the prince's representative visits your palace."

"You shouldn't have to be here if you don't want to be."

"Unfortunately, I don't always get to decide what I can or can't do. It comes with the territory and working for Berith."

Zeno fell silent. Sabin was pretty sure he knew what Zeno was thinking. He despised this place, having to talk to so many people and pretending to enjoy it. He didn't like crowds, so this evening was pretty much his worst nightmare.

Things weren't like this at the palace, but they were similar. Berith didn't have as many parties, but he did have to meet a lot of people, and of course, the palace was home to many demons. And when there *were* parties, it was unavoidable to have to attend. It would look bad for Berith if Sabin wasn't there, and Sabin never wanted to do anything that could hurt his friend.

But that kind of life was everything Zeno hated. It was everything he didn't want, and whatever hope Sabin had that Zeno might decide to stay at the palace with him once they got back fizzled out.

He'd been thinking about mentioning something to Zeno, and he'd been hopeful that Zeno would want to see where their relationship could go, but tonight had reinforced the fact that this wasn't Zeno's world. He was better on his own or with a few select people he loved. He'd never play well with dignitaries and other visiting demons. The palace wasn't his home, just like the desert wasn't Sabin's, and Sabin had been an idiot to think that could ever change.

And they were going home soon. They had a few more towns to visit on their way back to the palace, but they'd be short visits, and they'd be nothing like tonight. The earl was the most prominent demon in this area of Berith's territory, which was why everything was so polished around here. Zeno would be able to relax once they hit the road again, and he wouldn't be as tense in the small towns they still had to visit as he was tonight.

Sabin wanted to run back home, but at the same time, he never wanted to go back to the palace. The sooner he got back, the sooner he'd be with his friends and family again, and he'd return to his life. That also meant that he'd lose Zeno, though, and he wasn't ready for that.

But he also couldn't stay in the desert forever. No matter how much time he spent there, he still hated it with a passion.

So, what were they supposed to do?

"Do you have to go back inside?" Zeno asked.

Sabin did, but he didn't want to. "In a bit. Can you just hold me?"

"Whatever you need."

Sabin wished Zeno could give him that, but for now, this was enough. When it wasn't anymore, he'd deal with it.

Zeno's skin crawled at the thought of so many people being close to him. He wanted to drag Sabin back to the room they shared, pack their bags, and get back on the road before anyone could see them.

Unfortunately, Sabin had no way out of this party, which meant they were both stuck here. At least they'd gotten away from the earl who thought he could touch Sabin. Zeno had almost strangled him, but he'd managed to keep himself in check. This was important to Berith, which meant it was important to Sabin, and Zeno didn't want to ruin anything for him.

But breaking a few of the earl's fingers was really fucking tempting.

Zeno didn't understand how Sabin had gotten so deep under his skin in such a short time. He'd never felt the way he felt for Sabin, and he didn't know how to deal with it. He had no idea what to do, either. He wanted to be with Sabin, but he didn't see how it could be possible no matter how he looked at the situation. Sabin's home was the palace, while Zeno's was the desert. How could they make that work?

Allowing himself to grow so close to Sabin had been a bad idea. Now he was hooked, and he had no idea how to behave or what he'd do in the future. He didn't want to lose this opportunity with Sabin because he was sure he'd never find it again, but how could he live in the palace? He'd have to leave his life behind, and while it was something he'd gladly do for Sabin, what would it mean for him? Even if he got used to life in the palace, what was he supposed to do there?

He was a mercenary. He wasn't a bodyguard or anything else. He also wouldn't allow Berith to pay for him, which meant he had to continue working. What was he supposed to do, then? Would Berith want to use him as a mercenary? Did he even have a use for him? Or would he be doing Sabin a favor?

Zeno's head hurt when he thought too much about this, so he pushed the thoughts away and focused on Sabin. They didn't have a lot of time left together tonight, not until they got back to their room. Then tomorrow, they'd be on the road again, and while they still had a few towns to visit, they'd be back at the palace in under a week. Zeno had managed to stop thinking about what would happen then, but he couldn't afford to anymore. No matter how much he thought about it, he didn't have a solution.

He cleared his throat. "I'm sorry I growled at the earl," he muttered.

Sabin laughed. The sound was light and happy, and Zeno wanted to hear more of it. He never wanted Sabin to feel in a way that would make it impossible for him to laugh like this.

"I'm not. He was taking liberties he shouldn't have taken, and he should have known better. I don't know if he decided to ignore the fact that I wasn't into it or if he believed I was behaving like that to entice him even more, or maybe because I need to look like my only focus is Berith. Either way, he's an idiot, and I'm glad you stepped in."

"As long as it didn't ruin your work."

"It hasn't. I don't want you to worry about that. If the earl has a problem with what happened tonight, he's welcome to tell Berith about it. I'll be more than happy to let him handle it, but somehow, I don't think the earl would be. Berith wouldn't take what he's done any better than you have."

That was why Zeno liked Berith. He was a good friend, and he had strong ethics. He wouldn't have hesitated to step in to help Sabin, and that helped Zeno feel less guilty. Berith wouldn't want Sabin to compromise with the kind of demon who thought he could touch him without his consent.

Loud laughter made both of them turn. Sabin sighed, but he didn't move. "We should probably head back inside," he said.

"Is that what you want?"

"It couldn't be further from what I want, but eventually, I'll have to, if anything, to say goodbye."

"This has been the worst stop in this entire trip." At least for Zeno. He knew Sabin had enjoyed being back in a palace, having the opportunity to bathe and eat good food and everything else that came with the palace.

But to his surprise, Sabin nodded. "I agree. I can't wait to leave tomorrow."

"I can't believe you're happy to get back on the road."

"I can't say I am, but at least there, I don't have to fake-smile and go along with whatever the earl wants. Honestly, dealing with these people has been the worst part of this trip. I have to keep a smile on my face and nod, even though I want to scream and run out. I can't say I love the desert, but there's something to be said about there being no idiots there."

Zeno barked out a laugh. "There are plenty of idiots in the

desert."

"And the desert gets rid of them." Sabin shrugged. "I'll be glad to leave tomorrow morning."

"We'll go as soon as it's acceptable for us to."

"I agree."

Zeno looked for something else to say, but Sabin leaned closer and kissed him before he could. This wasn't the time and place, but Zeno didn't care. The earl could have barged in on them and demanded an explanation, and he wouldn't have cared. He had Sabin in his arms, and that was all that mattered, always.

Sabin had become the center of Zeno's world over the time they'd spent together, and Zeno wasn't sure how he'd be able to lose that center. He knew he didn't have to, and he'd be welcome to stay at the palace if he wanted. He was tempted, but at the same time, he was terrified that eventually he'd come to resent Sabin for trapping him there.

Of course, it wouldn't be Sabin trapping him. If he decided to stay at the palace, it would be his decision, not Sabin's. But he'd be staying for Sabin, and he needed to keep that in mind. He never wanted to be angry at Sabin or to hate him.

But he still didn't know what to do.

He supposed there was still time. They'd be on the road for several days still, and while it wasn't easy to think about this kind of thing, Zeno would have to deal with it. By the time they reached the palace, he'd have to have made a decision, whether he wanted to or not.

He still had no idea which way he'd go. His heart was torn in half, and for the first time ever, he had no idea how to get out of the trouble he'd gotten himself into.

CHAPTER EIGHTEEN

Sabin couldn't help the smile that stretched his lips when he finally stepped into the palace again. He was exhausted, he stank, and he couldn't wait to sleep in his bed, but none of that mattered, because he was home.

Cyarea cried out and ran toward him. He crouched and opened his arms, and she barreled into them, wrapping herself around him. "You're back!" she yelled, making him wince from how close she was to his ear.

"I am."

"You're not leaving ever again," she declared.

"Aren't I? I don't think you're the one making that kind of decision, Miss."

Her expression was serious when she leaned back. "I'll be the prince after Daddy. I get to make those decisions."

Sabin looked up at Berith, who hovered behind his daughter. Berith gave Sabin a sheepish smile and shrugged, and Sabin's heart almost exploded with how much love he had for these people.

The trip hadn't been fun, but he'd enjoyed spending time with Zeno. That time was over, and now they both had to make decisions neither of them wanted to make. They'd both been silent on the last leg of their trip, with Tobal carrying most of the conversation. He was still happy-go-lucky, but he'd started looking at Zeno with a worried expression, so he had to know something was about to happen.

Sabin got to his feet and looked around for Zeno, but he was nowhere to be seen. He started panicking, and Berith came closer, wrapping his arms around him and pulling him close. "He didn't go far. He's behind one of the carts."

Sabin relaxed. Zeno hadn't left without saying goodbye.

Berith leaned back, but he didn't let go of Sabin. He held him at arm's length, staring down at him with a frown. "You look tired."

"You'd be tired, too, if you had to spend so much time in the desert and meet so many annoying people."

Berith's lips creased into a smile. "Was it that bad?"

"It was probably worse than what you imagine. I have to tell you what the earl tried to do."

Berith groaned. "He's one of my least favorite people. No work for you today, though."

"Are you *ordering* me not to work?"

"Exactly. Take the rest of the day off. I'm sure you can't wait to take one of your famous baths and have good food."

That much was true, but Sabin hugged Berith again before stepping away. "I'm glad to be home."

"Even though it means you could lose Zeno?"

Sabin didn't have to tell Berith what had happened between him and Zeno. Berith could tell, but he'd always been good at reading Sabin. They'd been friends for a long time, after all. "I'll deal with it when it happens," he murmured.

"Just remember that I'm here if you want to talk."

Sabin didn't want to start crying, so he nodded and stepped away from Berith. He looked around for Zeno, but he was nowhere to be seen.

Sabin's stomach dropped. Had he already left? Sabin hoped Zeno would at least say goodbye, but maybe not. Maybe he'd decided it would be easier for them if they didn't linger.

"He was talking to Lon," Berith said.

"Who was?" Sabin asked, even though he knew he wasn't fooling his friend.

"I'll make sure that we're told about it if he tries to leave."

"I don't want anyone to stop him if he does."

"All right. But at least you'll know."

Sabin felt bad about what seemed like spying on Zeno, but he needed to know if Zeno left. After what had happened between them, the least Zeno owed him was to tell him he didn't want to stick around. Sabin wouldn't berate him for that. If anything, he'd understand. He didn't want to stay in the desert indefinitely, either.

Berith wrapped an arm around Sabin's shoulders and guided him toward the private wing where Sabin and the rest of the family had their rooms. "Who was that guy with you? He's not a guard, and I don't recognize him."

"That's Tobal. He's Zeno's brother, and he decided to come with us so he and Zeno could spend time together."

"I didn't know Zeno had a brother."

"Foster brother. He told me about his past and his childhood, and it wasn't good. Actually, we'll have to talk about that and make changes."

"Later," Berith ordered. "And if Zeno's brother wants to stay at the palace, I'm more than happy to welcome him."

"You don't even know him."

"So? I can always do with more people on my side."

"He might not be."

Berith scowled. "I'm trying to do a good thing, so stop attempting to change my mind. Besides, there's already one person at the very least who wants to kill me. Even if Tobal wants the same, I doubt it would change much."

Sabin's stomach churned at the reminder. "Has Lon discovered anything about that?"

"No, and it's driving him nuts. But today, I don't want you to think about any of this. Go to your room, get a nap, and I'll see you tonight for dinner."

Sabin nodded, and when Berith let him go, he headed toward his room. He couldn't wait to get there, but at the same time, he wondered where Zeno was. Why had he vanished suddenly? Why wasn't he here with Sabin, ready to take a nap by his side? Had he decided it would be better if they went their separate ways?

Whatever happened, Sabin would corner him tonight after dinner. He wanted to know what was happening between them and Zeno's plans. It was no use to worry over them when he didn't know them. There would be enough to worry over tonight.

The first thing Sabin did once he was back in his room was to take a bath. He stayed in the water until it cooled, but he refused the servants' offer to fill it again. He could fall asleep in there, and he didn't want to drown.

Once he was clean, he had a snack, then he went to bed. He'd thought he'd easily fall asleep, but instead, he continued thinking about Zeno.

There was no way things between them could work, was there?

No matter how many times Sabin thought about it, he couldn't find a way. Zeno's place was in the desert. He disliked how ostentatious the palace and the people who lived here were. He absolutely hated having to live with so many people around him. Even if he agreed to stay, he'd be miserable, and that wasn't what Sabin wanted.

But Sabin also didn't want to move to the desert. It wasn't his home, and it never would be. He supposed he'd be fine taking road trips every so often, but living there permanently? The thought made him shudder in horror. He'd be just as miserable as Zeno would be if he stayed here.

Clearly, in their case, love wouldn't be enough.

Sabin rolled to his front and grabbed his pillow, hugging it tightly. He was in love with Zeno, but he had no idea how Zeno felt about him. He suspected that Zeno at the very least liked him a lot, but was it love? And even if it was, what would it change?

Sabin supposed that how Zeno felt didn't matter. What he

felt for Zeno didn't, after all. They'd be separated over the next few days, and Sabin doubted he'd ever see Zeno again.

He sat up. If tonight was the last night he and Zeno would have, he wanted to make the most out of it. They'd had sex a few times on the road, but they'd kept it light. It had been awkward to do it in beds that didn't belong to them and in which other people would eventually sleep. Now, they were home, and no one would ever use Sabin's bed but him. Sabin knew what he wanted to do with Zeno, and he'd make it happen. As long as Zeno wanted him as much as he wanted Zeno, it would be perfect.

Even though it wouldn't last.

He swallowed. He needed to stop thinking about tomorrow. His only focus should be tonight, and since he doubted he'd get his nap, he could get himself ready for whatever would happen in his bed tonight.

Zeno wouldn't know what hit him.

Zeno had a hard time believing that he wasn't uncomfortable, but apparently, having dinner with Sabin's family was okay with him now, even though it meant he'd be surrounded by people. He supposed that since he was close to Sabin, he considered them his family, too. The fact that Tobal was there helped, but even with all that, Zeno still had no idea what to do with Cyarea.

She was sitting opposite him at the table, and she was staring. She was so still and quiet that it gave Zeno the creeps, but he wasn't sure what to do about it. Was it normal for young children to be so silent? Was she afraid of him?

She hadn't seemed afraid the last time they'd seen each other, but Zeno didn't know how children worked. Was he even supposed to do something about it, or should he just let her stare without saying anything?

"Just ignore her," Mel said.

He was sitting next to Cyarea. They'd arrived together, but for the first time since Zeno had met her, she hadn't seemed interested in her father's consort. Instead, she'd been looking around for something, and when she hadn't found it, she'd sat at the table and hadn't moved since then.

"Why is she doing that?" Zeno asked, trying to keep his voice soft. He didn't want to offend the girl. She was her father's daughter, and he wouldn't be surprised if she tried to stab him with her fork.

Mel chuckled. "I think she's fascinated by you."

"Why?"

Mel's smile widened. "You sound surprised."

"That's because I am. I'm just me."

"And you kept Sabin safe the entire time you were on the road. I think she has a bit of hero worship happening. She was worried her uncle Sabin would be attacked again and relieved when you came back and she saw he was fine. She credited you for that, and I wouldn't be surprised if she decided she wants to be a bodyguard when she grows up."

"No," Cyarea suddenly said, startling Zeno. "I'll be the prince, like Daddy. But Zeno can be my bodyguard."

Zeno might not know anything about children, but he was charmed. Maybe it was because of the easy way she accepted him. She had no idea what he did for a living or that he'd killed so many people in his life, but something told him that even if she did, it wouldn't faze her. Children were usually curious about him and his hood but not afraid. Not that the parents were, and it was clear that Berith, Mel, and Aloise were okay with Zeno.

Berith came in, his focus on a tablet. Zeno had always thought human technology looked odd, but he didn't see it often. Few demons could afford to get them from the human realm and to set things up to make them work. Even here at the palace, most demons didn't use it, but Sabin's tablet seemed to be an extension of his hand. He hadn't brought it on their trip because he wouldn't have been able to use it, but he'd lamented that fact several times while they were on the road.

"No tablets at the table," Mel drawled.

Berith looked up, blinking. "What?"

"You know the rules. No tablet at the table."

Berith kissed the top of Mel's head and sat next to him. "That rule was for Sabin, not for me."

"Nope. It was for both of you, so give me that."

Berith grinned. "What will you do if I don't?"

"It's more what I *won't* do if you don't."

Berith handed over his tablet so quickly that he almost hit Mel with it. Zeno had to bite on the inside of his lip so he wouldn't laugh. Berith was nothing like he'd imagined, and he suspected that was partly thanks to Mel. Zeno hadn't known Berith before he met the human, but he liked what he saw now.

"Where's Sabin?" Berith asked as he looked around.

Sabin was the only one missing now. Aloise was on Cy-area's other side, talking to Lon, who was sitting in front of her. Tobal was next to the head of security, and even though he wasn't talking much, he was listening to their conversation and nodding at whatever they were saying.

The only empty chair was the one next to Zeno's.

"I haven't seen him since he and the others arrived," Mel explained. "Maybe he's still asleep? We could send someone to knock on his door and make sure he's coming to dinner."

Before they could do that — and before Zeno volunteered to do it because he wanted to make sure Sabin was all right — the door opened again. Zeno twisted to see who it was, and his jaw dropped.

Sabin had arrived.

Most of the time he and Zeno had spent together, they'd been on the road. Sabin had done his best to clean up any time he'd had an opportunity, but even when he'd managed to get a bath at the earl's palace, he'd only had limited clothing with him. He'd been beautiful at the earl's party, but he was everything Zeno could have dreamed of right now.

Sabin's long purple hair was loose around his face. It looked softer than Zeno had ever seen it, and it made him want to touch it. Sabin's purple eyes were lined with black, making them look bigger and deeper. He wore a loose white tunic that fluttered around his legs as he strode toward the chair next to Zeno's. Zeno could smell his perfume when he sat, and he found himself leaning closer without thinking about it.

Sabin turned to him and gave him a blinding smile. "You look better."

Zeno had to swallow before he could say anything. "You look beautiful."

Sabin's smile turned satisfied. "I know, thank you."

Zeno had no words. He couldn't look away from Sabin, and he was so focused that the servant placing a plate in front of him on the table startled him.

Dinner felt like it lasted forever. Zeno couldn't focus on anything or anyone that wasn't Sabin, and by the time it was over, he wasn't sure what he'd eaten. He was sure everything had been delicious, but none of it mattered.

Only Sabin did.

Sabin got to his feet as they were finishing dessert. "Well, I'm headed to bed."

"Already?" Mel said. There was teasing in his voice, and his gaze bounced from Sabin to Zeno as if he knew something Zeno didn't.

"I'm still tired from the trip. Aren't you tired, too, Zeno?"

Zeno knew what Sabin was doing, and he couldn't resist. "I'll walk you to your rooms."

It was easy to ignore the stares and the giggles. Zeno didn't look at anyone, not even at Tobal. He offered Sabin his arm, and Sabin took it with a smile.

That smile only lasted until they got to the hallway.

The dining room door closed behind them, and Sabin was on Zeno. He pushed into Zeno's arms and kissed him, and Zeno could only take it.

He did so with pleasure.

He groaned into Sabin's mouth, very aware of where they were but not caring one bit. That changed when the dining room door opened and a servant stepped out. Her eyes widened when she saw them, and she quickly retreated back into the room. That was enough for Zeno to decide that he and Sabin needed to move.

He gently pushed Sabin away, grabbed his hand before he could think Zeno was rejecting him, and dragged him down the hallway. Sabin's laughter rang high and happy, hitting Zeno right in the feels. He wanted to keep this, and his heart hurt at the thought that he couldn't.

But he didn't want to think about that right now. His only focus tonight should be Sabin, and that was what he'd force himself to do. He could think about what came next and the pain it would bring later. He wouldn't ruin this night for either of them.

He didn't slow down even when they reached Sabin's rooms. He pushed the door open, pulled Sabin in, and slammed the door shut with a foot. Then he made a beeline for Sabin's bedroom.

And froze.

Sabin had clearly expected him to come back with him, and he'd planned for it. The bed was perfectly made, the sheets clean and fresh. Dozens of candles lit the room, and a soft breeze came from the open windows. It carried the sweet scent of desert flowers, and it threw Zeno right back to the field where he and Sabin had first been together.

"I didn't want to assume, but I hoped you'd come back with me," Sabin murmured.

Zeno didn't care how the room looked. He only cared

about Sabin, and he turned to him, pulled him into his arms again, and kissed him.

The soft fabric of Sabin's clothing was a hindrance, but Zeno didn't want to tear it off him. Well, he did want to tear it off, but he wasn't willing to make Sabin angry, so instead, he pulled on it as gently as he could until he managed to get it off Sabin's body.

Sabin's tail gently swished behind him, but when Zeno grabbed Sabin's ass, it wrapped around one of his forearms. It didn't feel like Sabin was trying to stop him, so Zeno didn't stop. Instead, he splayed his hands on Sabin's ass and pried open his ass cheeks, sliding a finger between them.

And got the second surprise since they'd reached Sabin's rooms.

Sabin's hole was loose and slick. When Zeno pressed his fingertip against it, it easily slid in, and Sabin's body welcomed him. Sabin shuddered in his arms and buried his face against his chest, where Zeno could feel his warm breath through the light fabric of his tunic.

"Like I said, I hoped you'd come back with me," Sabin said.

Zeno wanted this moment to be perfect for Sabin, and he'd believed he could only achieve that by being a gentleman and taking it as slow as he could, but that wasn't him, and Sabin knew it. He wouldn't expect it from him, and it was time for Zeno to be himself. That was the Zeno Sabin had fallen in love with, after all.

He hauled Sabin into his arms, smiling at the squeak Sabin gave. He didn't protest, though, not even when Zeno dumped him onto the bed. He was beautiful against the white sheets, and for tonight, he was Zeno's.

Zeno wanted to stare at Sabin for the rest of the night, but instead, he quickly undressed. He dumped his clothes on the floor, not caring one bit where they ended up. He'd never been self-conscious about the way he looked, but now that he was naked in front of Sabin, he found himself hesitating.

"Don't," Sabin said.

"What?"

"You're beautiful."

Zeno knew that wasn't true. He had scars—many of them—and part of one of his horns was missing. But here, in front of Sabin, he *felt* beautiful.

Sabin wasn't lying. He loved the way Zeno looked, but more importantly, he loved Zeno, and that was all that mattered to him.

He could tell the instant Zeno realized that the way he looked didn't matter. His expression smoothed out, and he finally lowered his body on top of Sabin's. Sabin wished he'd had more time to look at Zeno, but that was fine. He'd do it later.

And there was so much to look at.

Instead, Sabin ran his fingers down Zeno's spine, feeling the hard bumps that protruded from his skin. Zeno's cock was hard and had slid out of the pouch at his groin, and it was pressed against Sabin's. That wasn't where Sabin wanted it, though, so he wiggled until it slipped between his ass cheeks. He'd made sure to be ready for this because he was done waiting, and now, the moment had come.

He grinned when the head of Zeno's cock hit his hole. A little bit more wiggling and some help from Zeno, who looked at Sabin with a fond expression, and Zeno's cock was finally sliding in.

They became one. It had never been quite the same with anyone else, and Sabin didn't expect it to ever be like this again if it wasn't with Zeno. Zeno moved slowly but surely, strength in his every thrust.

Sabin wrapped his tail around Zeno's back, holding him close. His own cock was painfully hard, and the friction of his and Zeno's bodies pressed together didn't help. When the tip pushed into the top of Zeno's pouch, Sabin cried out. He clung to Zeno so hard that he wouldn't be surprised to find signs from his nails on Zeno's back.

Zeno gave Sabin a wicked grin and angled his hips so that the next time he thrust into Sabin, Sabin's cock pushed into his pouch. It was too much—too many sensations, too many emotions. Sabin didn't know what to focus on, so he let go instead of trying and failing. Zeno would catch him when he fell.

He did. He held Sabin as the orgasm hit, and Sabin shuddered in his arms. He continued moving inside of Sabin, more slowly and deeply now, until it was Sabin's time to hold him. Sabin liked it—he liked when Zeno took care of him, but he also wanted to take care of Zeno. He suspected no one ever had, and he was touched to be the one person Zeno allowed close enough.

But when it was over and Zeno rolled to his side, Sabin ended up in his arms. It was a mirror position of the one they'd been in when they'd been on the road, and it was so familiar that Sabin felt his eyelids close before he was ready to fall asleep. He wanted to spend more time with Zeno, and he tried to sit up, but Zeno held him where he was.

"Sleep," he whispered.

Sabin obeyed.

CHAPTER NINETEEN

Zeno couldn't stop looking at Sabin. He was asleep, looking more peaceful than Zeno had ever seen him. They'd shared a bed when they'd been on the road, but Sabin had always been tense. He'd been far from home in places where he didn't feel secure or comfortable, and that had been obvious. This morning, though, he was where he belonged, and Zeno couldn't take him away.

He sighed and wiggled to see if Sabin would roll away. He was tucked against Zeno's side, his face pressed against Zeno's chest. They'd shared enough beds for Zeno to know that Sabin would roll to the other side if he moved too much. He did so in his sleep, so hopefully, he wouldn't notice when Zeno snuck out of bed and his bedroom.

Zeno stared at Sabin for one last moment. He wanted to remember this instant forever, even though it would hurt to know he couldn't have it again. They'd both be miserable if they had to make compromises, so, unfortunately, it meant that they had to go their own separate ways. It felt like the hardest thing Zeno had ever done, harder even than leaving Tobal behind. Now, he had Tobal back, but he was losing Sabin.

He stared at the ceiling and wiggled again. Obsessing over what was about to happen wouldn't help anyone, least of all him. Sabin would be pissed when he woke up and found out that Zeno had snuck out, but Zeno didn't care. He needed to leave, and he didn't want to say goodbye.

What had happened last night was enough goodbye, and

he hoped Sabin would understand eventually. Having Sabin walk him to the palace entrance and wave at him as he disappeared into the crowd would only hurt more than the thought of leaving.

Sabin grunted and rolled away, just like Zeno had expected. Sabin's dark purple hair was spread over the pillow, a soft cloud that surrounded his face. It took everything Zeno had to tear himself away, and when he did, he wanted to go back with every step he took. Instead, he gathered his clothes and headed toward the door, quietly putting them on once he was in the sitting area. Then he opened the door and snuck into the hallway.

The sound of the door closing behind him was final and reverberated down his spine. This was it. He was leaving the palace and Sabin, and he'd never be back.

Every step he took toward his room was heavy. He knew he'd find Tobal there, since he'd told him to stay in his room while he was with Sabin. He hoped Tobal would come with him, but he wasn't sure, and that worried him, too. He couldn't force Tobal to do anything, and he didn't want to, anyway.

But he was starting to realize that it might be better to keep everyone away. If he never cared for anyone, he wouldn't be hurt when he lost them.

He was careful when he pushed his bedroom door open. He peeked in, not one bit surprised to see Tobal sitting on the bed, his legs crossed under him as he ate breakfast. Tobal looked up, grinning at Zeno until he noticed Zeno's expression. Then his smile turned into a frown. "What happened?"

"Nothing. I'm perfectly fine."

"Sure you are. That's why you look like your dog died."

"I don't have a dog."

"Who cares. What's going on?"

Zeno headed for the bathroom. His brother followed him, but then, he'd always been like a hellhound when he wanted answers. He clung until Zeno gave him what he wanted, and in this case, it was for Zeno to talk.

"I'm leaving," he declared.

The frown was still there, firm on Tobal's face. "What do you mean?"

"Exactly what I said."

"But what about Sabin? Didn't you just spend the night with him?"

"I did."

"Aren't the two of you together? I'm confused."

Zeno didn't want to explain, but he felt he owed it to his brother. "We were together, yes. But let's face it, it could never work between us. He's a palace boy, and I can't stand living with so many people. He can't stand the desert, where I'm happier. How are things supposed to work between us?"

"And you're just going to give up?"

"I don't see it as giving up. I see it as trying my best to make both of us happy."

Tobal snorted. He was leaning against the doorframe, his arms crossed over his chest. "And you really think that sneaking out early in the morning will make Sabin happy? Or you, for that matter."

"We won't be happy right away. It will hurt, but we'll come out of it eventually."

Tobal didn't say anything, but Zeno could feel his brother's gaze on him. He ignored it as he finished washing up, not one bit embarrassed that he was naked. After what he and Tobal had gone through together, nakedness was the last thing they worried about.

Once Zeno was clean, he headed back to the bedroom. He hadn't unpacked his things from the road trip, so it was easy for him to find a pair of pants and a tunic to wear in the desert. He put them on, then packed everything he'd owned when he'd first arrived in the bag. After he was done, there were no signs that he'd ever lived in this room. He supposed that wasn't surprising, considering he hadn't been here long.

"So you're leaving," Tobal said quietly.

"I am."

"What about me?"

Zeno briefly closed his eyes before facing his brother. "I'd like for you to come with me. I don't want to lose you so soon after finding you again, but I can't force you to do anything. If you want to stay, I'll understand."

"Even me staying here won't convince you to stay."

"I can't be happy living in this room and having to deal with so many people every day." Sometimes, he wondered if he was broken. He wouldn't be surprised if that was the case after what he'd been put through when he was a child.

Tobal sighed heavily. "Dammit. I was looking forward to living at the palace, but I guess I'll come with you."

Zeno's chest tightened. "You don't have to. I told you about my life. It's not for everyone, and I don't expect you to live it." He'd wanted Tobal to know that he was The Mercenary and that he couldn't afford *not* to be. It was the only thing he knew how to do.

"I'm not saying I'm going to help you with your job, but the least I can do is travel with you. I can't promise I'll move into your shack after the way you described it, but I don't want us to go our separate ways yet. I'm not ready to lose you again."

The relief was almost enough to knock Zeno to his knees. "We can go whenever you're ready."

"I guess I am. It's not like I have anything to pack. Let me dress and grab my bag."

Zeno wanted to give his brother all the time he needed to get ready, but he was nervous. Eventually, Sabin would wake up, and he'd be pissed when he couldn't find Zeno. If Zeno was anywhere near the palace when that happened, he'd have to face Sabin's wrath and probably Berith's, too. He suspected there was no coming back from that, so the sooner he got out, the better it would be.

But this morning, Tobal was as slow as a fire slug. He took his time in the bathroom, then dressed and packed his bag. Once that was done, they had to go to the kitchen to get food that would last them long enough for the first part of their trip.

Zeno's skin crawled as he got more and more anxious. He needed to get out of here, and he needed to go now. Every second he spent at the palace made him want to stay, even though he'd be miserable if he did. The best thing for everyone was for him to go, and the only way that would happen was if Tobal finally stopped wasting time.

Sabin knew he was alone as soon as he opened his eyes. He shot up in bed, frantically looking around for Zeno, but he couldn't see him anywhere. His heart raced as he threw himself out of bed, his legs tangling in the sheet. He fell off the bed, but even though it hurt, he had better things to do than cry over it. He grabbed the sheet, pulled it off the bed, and wrapped it around his body as he headed for the door.

He had no idea when Zeno had left, but if he was lucky, he'd manage to get to him before he got out of the palace. Once he did, he'd yell at him for leaving without talking to him.

He ran down the hallway, not caring about who he startled. A few servants screamed as if they'd never seen him act this way.

To be fair, they hadn't. Usually Sabin was the voice of reason and Berith was the one who did stupid things like falling in love with a human. This time around, it was Sabin who'd fallen in love with the most inconvenient demon, and as soon as he found that damn demon, he was going to kick his ass. He didn't care that he had no experience when it came to fighting. He'd make sure Zeno knew what he thought about him sneaking out.

A door opened just as Sabin ran past it. He barreled against the demon who came out, but thankfully for him, the demon managed to catch him. When Sabin looked up, it was into Berith's startled gaze.

"Sorry about that," he said as he shook off Berith's hands.

"Not a problem. But what's going on?"

"I need to get to the entrance. Zeno is gone."

Berith swore. Thankfully, he didn't ask for more of an explanation or whether Sabin was sure. Instead, he grabbed Sabin's hand and pulled him down the hallway, running along with him.

Sabin squeezed his friend's hand. He didn't know what would happen with Zeno, but whatever the outcome would be, he'd always have Berith. Sabin would never be alone, and if he had his heart broken, Berith and Lon would make sure it healed. Eventually, it would have to, right?

"When did you last see him?" Berith asked.

"Last night."

"You spent the night together?"

"Yes."

Berith glanced at Sabin. "I guess that explains the toga."

"I didn't have time to get dressed."

"As long as you don't flash anyone, I don't have a problem with what you're wearing. Now, where do you think Zeno is?"

Sabin stumbled. Where could Zeno be? "It depends. I have no idea when he left my bedroom, so he could be anywhere, from the kitchens to the desert."

Berith tightened his hold on Sabin's hand. "Don't think about that. Think that he's still around and that we'll find him."

They startled a guard as he turned a corner, and Berith pointed his finger at the demon. "You. Make sure no one leaves the palace."

The guard straightened. "Your Majesty?"

"Don't hurt anyone." Berith was still running, and now, the guard was running beside him and Sabin.

Sabin felt ridiculous, and he could only imagine what their little group looked like. He was mortified, but Zeno mattered more than feeling ashamed of the spectacle he was making.

"We're looking for Zeno."

"He was headed toward the back entrance, your Majesty," the guard said. "We crossed paths earlier."

"How long ago was that?" Sabin asked. His heart raced as if it knew that Zeno was gone.

"About five minutes? He can't have gone far."

Berith clapped the guard's shoulder with his free hand, then pulled Sabin along. "Come on."

If Sabin hadn't been running to catch up to Zeno, he'd have stopped, but he couldn't. Right now, the only thing that mattered was Zeno. If Sabin managed to get to him, he might be able to change Zeno's mind. And if he didn't, well, all of this would have been for nothing, but at this point, he didn't care.

They stumbled out of the door in the secondary entrance courtyard. This was the entrance the servants used, and the gate was much smaller than the main one. There were guards there, and just as Sabin saw them, they opened the gates to let Zeno and Tobal through.

"Zeno!" Sabin yelled.

Zeno's back went ramrod straight. He'd clearly thought Sabin wouldn't notice he was gone until he was far from the palace, but he'd been wrong, and Sabin felt a savage satisfaction.

He and Berith came to a stop in front of Zeno and his brother. Tobal looked amused, but it was impossible to read Zeno's expression, because his hood was up. Sabin let go of Berith's hand and pushed the hood down. Zeno didn't protest, and Sabin took a moment to catch his breath.

"What are you doing?" Zeno asked.

Sabin raised a hand so Zeno would know he needed a

moment to catch his breath. "Finding your stupid ass," he panted.

"You should still be asleep."

"And you should still be in my bed." The sheet started to slide down Sabin's shoulder, and he angrily pulled it up. "What were you thinking? We haven't even talked about this."

"What's there to talk about? We both know we can't be together. You hate the desert, and there's no way you'll want to stay there for longer than a road trip, but I can't stand living at the palace with so many people around me."

"You two are idiots," Berith declared behind them.

Sabin blinked and turned to look at him. "You're not going to help us by insulting us."

"Maybe not, but I feel like it's justified, because you're idiots."

"What are you talking about?" Sabin asked, throwing his hands up. He gave up. He hated both Berith and Zeno, and that was that.

"The gardens," Berith said.

Both Zeno and Sabin stared at him. It was good to know that Sabin wasn't the only one confused.

Berith chuckled. "Think about it. Zeno, your problem is that you don't want to live at the palace, right? There are too many people around, and you feel awkward around servants."

"Yes," Zeno agreed. "I'm used to being on my own, and that's never going to happen here."

Berith dismissed him and turned his attention to Sabin. "And you. You can't imagine a life away from the palace and your bathtub."

"And you, you asshole. You're one of my best friends. I don't want to lose you."

Berith nodded, clearly satisfied if his smile was an indication of anything. "So, we'll build you a house in the garden."

Sabin still didn't understand. "What are you talking about?"

"You know how far the gardens go. We leave most of it untouched because it would take too much work and money, which means that the parts further away from the palace are wild, and no one goes there. It wouldn't take much to cut down a bunch of trees and build you a house. We'll include the biggest tub we can get in there and create a path between the house and the palace. You can put a gate and walls or whatever if you want to make sure people don't bother you, but Sabin will be close enough to the palace to come to work every morning, while Zeno will be isolated enough that he won't feel crowded and anxious."

Sabin stared. He'd never thought about that and didn't understand why or how Berith had. He wanted to thank him, but nothing he could say or do would be enough.

"What do you think?" Berith asked. His attention was on Zeno since he'd been the one leaving.

Sabin faced him, holding his breath. Whatever Zeno was about to say, it might heal or break his heart.

"You really think this house can be isolated enough?" he asked.

Berith nodded. "I promise you it will be. I'll show you the place I was thinking about if you want, but you won't have to see anyone for days if you don't want to."

Zeno turned his gaze to Sabin. "Then I accept."

EPILOGUE

Sabin jumped over the stream, his hooves making noise as they landed on the path. He grinned, his heart lighter than it ever had been. The gardens surrounding him were beautiful, and he couldn't believe he had the opportunity to live here, in a place he always felt was his.

Well, his and Zeno's now.

Sabin could already see the roof of the little house they shared deep in the garden. The path would take him straight there, and even though the wilderness hid it in some spots, he knew his way home. Right there, in that house, Zeno was waiting for him.

Things hadn't been easy. Even with all the resources that Berith had at his disposal, it had taken a few months to build the house. Berith had gone all out and insisted on paying for it, even though it made Zeno uncomfortable. Sabin had long gotten used to Berith using his money for his friends, and he'd stopped trying to convince him to do otherwise. Berith would always do what Berith wanted, and that was that.

Zeno had been anxious the whole time it took to build the house. Some days, the palace got to be too much for him, and he disappeared into the desert for hours. Sabin was worried that he wouldn't come back, but he always had, and now he wasn't going anywhere ever again. He was home, just like Sabin was.

Sabin couldn't have imagined anything like this happening to them. Even when he'd realized he loved Zeno, he'd thought he would eventually lose him, and he would have if Berith hadn't come up with this plan. Now, Sabin could walk to the palace every morning and back home every evening.

Sometimes Zeno was there to welcome him, while the house was empty at other times. Zeno wasn't working as much as he had before, and now, he mostly took his orders from Berith. At the moment, he and Lon were working together to find out who kept letting demons in, but they hadn't had any success, and it was starting to make them nervous and angry. Luckily, no one had attempted to attack Berith for months, but it was only a question of time.

Sabin smiled when he saw the lights were on in the house. He moved faster, but the front door had already swung open by the time he reached it. Zeno was waiting for him, a smile that he reserved for Sabin stretching his lips.

"You're late," he said.

"I'm sorry. I got caught up with Berith, and you know how he is when he starts talking."

Zeno laughed and wrapped an arm around Sabin's waist. He pulled him against his chest, and Sabin relaxed.

He was home.

"I love you," he told Zeno.

Zeno's eyes sparkled. "And I love you."

Neither of them had thought they could make things work, but they had, and that was all that mattered. They'd been ready to make the hardest choice they could have made, and Zeno had when he tried sneaking out of the palace. They wouldn't be here if it weren't for Berith, and Sabin had never been so happy to have him as one of his best friends.

They would find the demons trying to kill him, and they would make sure nothing happened to him.

But that was something he didn't have to think about now. The only thing he had to worry about was what Zeno had in mind as he dragged him into the house and slammed the door behind them.

ABOUT THE AUTHOR

Catherine is the creator of several series, most of them paranormal, including the Whitedell Pride Series and the Gillham Pack Series. While she graduated in translation, she decided to go the writer's way because it was more fun to create her own stories and characters.

She's been living in Italy for more than twenty years, but she's a daughter of the North—Belgium to be precise—and she misses it so much that she's already planning to move back.

She loves pizza—probably too much —her son, her pets, and of course, books. She sneaks some reading time into her schedule every time she has five minutes free from writing, demands from her various pets and son, and lastly, housework.

Connect with her:

lievens.catherine@gmail.com
BookBub: https://www.bookbub.com/authors/catherine-lievens
Website: https://authorcatherinelievens.com/
Facebook: https://www.facebook.com/catherine.lievens.9
Facebook Group: https://www.facebook.com/groups/411788002341528/
Twitter: https://twitter.com/authorCLievens
Newsletter: http://eepurl.com/c-uvKn

www.ingramcontent.com/pod-product-compliance
Lightning Source LLC
Chambersburg PA
CBHW070828120626

46556CB00002B/681